The
Whirligig
of Time

Books by Isabel Bolton

Novels:
Do I Wake or Sleep?
The Christmas Tree
Many Mansions

A Memoir:
Under Gemini

The
Whirligig
of Time

a novel by
ISABEL BOLTON

Crown Publishers, Inc., New York

To Virginia Stevens
with love and gratitude

CHAPTER

1

OLD DAVID HARE turned the leaves of the telephone book. (Was she, he wondered, listed? She might for all he knew be dead.) W—Wi—Willoughby—Willoughby, A.—here it was—Willoughby, Blanche—78 West Fourth Street. Where the devil was West Fourth Street?

Spring 4-6798. He rang the number. "Hello, hello, is this Miss Willoughby's apartment?"

"Yes, this is Miss Willoughby. With whom am I speaking?"

"Blanche, do you know my voice?"

A moment's hesitation. "David! Can it possibly be you?"

"Am I forgiven, Blanche?"

"Ten thousand times, my dear, ten thousand times."

"When can I come to see you—tomorrow?"

"Not tomorrow, I must have a tooth out. But the next day, David."

"At what time, Blanche?"

"At four," she said and hung up the receiver.

He knew that she was weeping, and visibly moved himself, left the telephone and went to the dressing table, where he stood looking at his reflection in the mirror. Had he changed greatly? Would she know him if she met him on the street? That scar across his face, a casualty of the First World War, certainly had not improved his appearance. But he was vigorous still, though his hair and his moustache were white. He still resembled his great-uncle Alexander, but was not nearly so distinguished.

Leaving the mirror, he turned on the television and sat down before it. Knights of interstellar space, voyages to the moon. Could anyone persuade him to believe that he was actually listening to their voices, watching them perform their unimaginable feats—here in this room, before his very eyes? God!

He went to the window—there before him was his native city—towers behind towers, pinnacles, terraces, setbacks, and at a lower level, edifices of stronger, squarer structure—citadels of glass and iron, where how many millions lived like bees in their familiar hives. What if from some well-calculated altitude? Brrr! He lifted his shoulders, hunching them as though to shield himself from entering such awful areas of speculation. Above, a jet plane streaked, roaring across the sky. Whither bound? Istanbul? Tel Aviv? Nairobi?—an easy stride.

And then—retreating—turning his back on centuries of change, he heard the rumble of carriage wheels, the clip, clip, clip of horses' hoofs upon the pavement. He inhaled the smell of horse manure, of paving stones drenched in dust and sunshine. The sky was an uninterrupted blue above his head. He was in a neighborhood, solid, accustomed, friendly, where houses were of uniform height and aspect. There were hansom cabs, broughams, ladies alighting from victorias, calling cases in hand; gentlemen in frock coats and silk hats climbed the steps of brownstone houses. Mr. Wildering's brougham was waiting in front of his large house at the corner of Thirty-sixth and Park, and accompanied by Olivia he got into the carriage and allowed the footman to place a robe around their knees.

He was walking down the avenue holding his mother's hand. They were on their way to the park at the corner of Park Avenue and Thirty-fourth Street, with the iron fence around it and the gates admitting only those families who by right of birth or bank account were privileged to enter.

The sound of children's voices, children's laughter, sunlight and shadow on the grass, the winding walks, nursemaids pushing baby carriages; bonnes and fräuleins admonished in French and German. Little boys dashed in and out on roller skates, little girls behind runaway hoops hit them vigorously with their hoop sticks, mothers sat on benches reading or chatting with their neighbors. The fountain played, the wind blew the spray, sparrows hopped and chattered, pigeons crooned and strutted and pecked—voices, voices, children's laughter. Was it autumn, with the smell of burning leaves upon the air, dry leaves shuffled under children's feet, or was it winter, the walks swept clean of snow and here, and there a lane of ice on which the children slid and tumbled, snow covering the grass, children shouting, throwing snowballs, or was it spring, when Mr. Pierson's bull occupied the southeast corner of the park and the big sign was out to advertise his presence—Do Not Notice Bull—when the air was full of music, hurdy-gurdies, barrel-organs, and when at noon the old man with his organ and his monkey arrived at the northwest gate and ground out "Sweet Mary O'Grady," while his little monkey, dressed in velvet, took off his tiny hat and extending his long arm through the iron bars, begged for pennies from the children assembled on the other side?

Voices, voices, children's names on the air. How many of them now did he remember? Lily and Blanche, of course, Anna Budinot, the Ware boys, their little sister—was she Lucy, was she Jane? Emmet Harris and Olivia Wildering.

Above all, he thought of Olivia. Had she not been, as far back as he remembered, the little princess of the park? "Thank Miss Olivia for her ball. It was very kind of her to let you have it, Master David."

Ghosts, ghosts, a procession of ghosts, memories, voices. . . .

Old Miss Willoughby was weeping when she laid down the receiver. She could not control herself. She had been so taken by surprise. And now David, whom she had expected never to see again, was here in New York and would, pending no dreadful consequences from that visit to the dentist, come on Thursday to see her. Making a great effort to control herself, she turned to Mrs. Drew, who had just entered with some letters on a tray.

"Why," the fatuous creature exclaimed, "what are we weeping for? Bursting into tears because we have to have our tooth pulled!"

"How absurd, I am not bursting into tears because I'm going to the dentist. I've had a great and unexpected shock."

"I hope no one has died."

"Oh no, no, quite the contrary." And bursting into tears again, Miss Willoughby attempted to explain herself. "Only an old friend, a dear friend I haven't seen in over fifty years telephoned and told me he was in New York."

"A boyfriend! Well! That's the reason for our tears."

"He isn't a boyfriend. I never had a boyfriend and I dislike the word exceedingly."

"It's clear enough we're all upset, and I must add that I'm surprised to see the dignified Miss Willoughby reduced to tears, because, no, I won't say it again, a friend who seems to mean so much to her . . ."

Disgusted with herself for her irritability and feeling she could not tolerate Mrs. Drew's society a moment longer, old Miss Willoughby rose and went to the window.

The day was clear and beautiful. She saw the church of Our Lady of Pompeii with its dome and lifted cross, and from a neighboring rooftop pigeons ascending and a boy with a stick running about below them. Presently they descended and the boy shooed them off on another upward flight.

She loved her low-roofed skyscape and was always glad to have the great sky lanes and avenues of glass and concrete at her back. She had never grown accustomed to the city which she had watched growing up around her on the limitless pavement of the sky, and she wondered as she watched the pigeons descend again in scattered flight how this incredible metropolis would appear to David after his many years in exile.

She thought of David and of his mother, whom she had so deeply loved, and remembered a morning in that vanished park when her desperate little act, compelled by yearning and a great need for affection, had procured for her all she had ever known of love and joy, passion, pain, and sorrow, and a poignant sense of the bitter ironies of life.

How it all came back—that joyous participation in the spring—children calling to each other, voices on the air, the games, the sense that spring had come, buds bursting, blossoms opening, the young green leaves, the cool sweet wind of May—skipping her rope, hopping on one foot from square to square and knowing *she* was there, that beautiful lady whose presence or absence meant all the difference between content and bitter disappointment.

Had she not prayed all the way from Thirty-ninth Street: "Let her come, oh, God, please let her come with David to the park." And now how wonderful to feel that she could turn whenever she had the need to do so and watch her as she sat reading or knitting on her bench beneath the tulip tree.

But David's mother had never noticed her. She had not known her name as she knew the names of Jackie and Louisa Ware and Anna Budinot. If only she could do something to attract her attention—fall into the pond or break her collar-bone or maybe even just go up and sit beside her on the bench and wait until she spoke to her.

And so on that May day before she quite knew what she was about, she had left the children and gone, her knees trembling and her heart beating very fast, to the bench where she was sitting. And then summoning all her courage, had climbed up and sat beside her. She was reading and took no notice of her. She had wondered if she could touch her or even try to speak.

And then the beautiful lady, like the blessed damosel, leaned out from the gold bar of heaven, and inspecting her an instant, had said, "Who are *you?*"

How she had ever managed to answer, she didn't know, but she thought she heard herself reply that she was Blanche Willoughby.

"Willoughby, Willoughby." She seemed to be musing over something. And did she and her sister live on Thirty-ninth Street with their great-aunt, Miss Lydia Beekman?

"Yes, Mrs. Hare," she had whispered.

"Well, you know," the enchanting voice went on, "I think you're David's second or third or fourth cousin, several times removed perhaps."

She had no idea what it meant to be so many times removed, but she had said that she was some kind of cousin and the news seemed too remarkable even for her to believe. Could it be possible then that the lady of her dreams might be her cousin too? She had waited, and before anything more was said, Anna Budinot's mother had come gushing up to her and both were presently engaged in an endless conversation.

On they went. Her heart began to sink. Had she forgotten all about her? The conversation continued, and finally she climbed down from the bench and slowly walked away. This was the end of it all then. She would never think of her again. She might just as well have never gone to sit beside her.

But she had been wrong. David's mother had not forgotten her. The very next afternoon she had gone to call on her great-aunt, and on the following day she and her sister, Lily, had received an invitation to have supper with David in their house on Park Avenue.

And so it had all begun, going there so often and in what seemed no time at all becoming almost like members of the family, being always asked to all those wonderful Christmas and Easter and birthday celebrations. Life became full of love and friendliness, of strange excitements and beautiful events. What with all those remarkable people, the fascinating, the terrible Uncle Alexander, who said such startling things, and little Mr. Friedermann, who always played the piano after dinner, and Great-aunt Adelaide flourishing her ear trumpet and shrieking at everyone, and of course always the beloved cousin Laura, who was the core and center of her happiness.

The boy was still flying the pigeons, and a wedding party was coming out of Our Lady of Pompeii. Old Miss Willoughby, as she turned from the window, said to herself, or was she speaking to the beloved cousin Laura, "How beautiful you were. How I have loved you!"

THE OLD GENTLEMAN was unable to sleep. He was thinking about Blanche and of her great love for his mother. His sigh, heavy with memory and remorse, fetched up a name which, as music accompanies a song, always accompanied the thought of his mother.

Louise Denis (or was it Louis?), a goblin, a bugaboo name that for a long period in his childhood, had, whenever he heard it mentioned or so much as thought of it himself, seem d to threaten his happiness, his security, his home—all those familiar objects and occurrences that gave him a name and an identity—the chiming of the clock on the drawing room mantelpiece, the pictures on the walls, arrivals and departures, family festivals, the morning sunlight in the dining room, the flowery coffee cups, his mother's kiss and his father's reprimand.

"Louise Denis," he repeated, "Louise Denis." And there he seemed to be, a small boy on an autumn evening, looking out onto Park Avenue. The lamplighter was coming down the street, stopping on every corner to light the lamps. He was whipping himself up into a state of great anxiety. Why didn't his mother come home? She had told him she would be back early. A hansom clattered by. He heard his father come up the stoop, let himself in with his door key, and ascend the stairs to his library above.

Norah, the parlormaid, came in from the dining room carrying her long wand and lighted taper. She lighted up the chandelier in the back drawing room, and advancing to the front room lifted her wand to light the other chandelier.

"Why hasn't my mother come in?" he asked, as though she were responsible for the delay.

"She'll be in, in her good time," she said, coming to the window to draw down the shade.

"Leave the shade up, Norah," he demanded crossly.

"Please yourself," she said, and closing him in behind the heavy curtains, went to the other window to complete her task.

A brougham, ah! there she was, but no, it rumbled past. But who was that under the lamp across the street? Was it his mother? No, it could not be. She was talking to a gentleman with a pointed beard. But yes, it was his mother. He saw the gentleman stoop and kiss her and then turn into Thirty-sixth Street. She ran quickly across the street, up the sidewalk, and still hurrying, mounted the stoop and rang the bell.

Norah came to answer the bell and his father came down the stairs to greet her. He left his post behind the curtains and going to the threshold of the door into the hall, stopped short.

"Why are you late?" his father said. "I thought you took the carriage."

"No, I dismissed it," she said. "I walked home and stopped next door to call on Mrs. Phillips."

How could she lie, he thought, so quickly?

"But where is my little boy?" she asked. "Isn't he coming to give his mama a kiss?"

And now the dining room was full of sunlight. He slipped into his chair at the breakfast table. He was not going to speak to his mother. He did not even want to look at her. She was pouring the coffee and talking to his father, something about an invitation to a party. She stopped and told him they were going to have griddle cakes and maple syrup. He did not answer.

"Take your elbows off the table," his father reprimanded.

"My dear," he heard her tell him, as she poured herself another cup of coffee, she was giving a small dinner party.

And his father had asked her, looking up from his paper, if she had not already finished paying off her social obligations?

Well, yes, she admitted, she had. But this was for a special purpose. She wanted a few friends to meet a very charming gentleman.

At this point he pricked up his ears and listened attentively, for his father was asking her the name of this very charming gentleman.

"Louis Denis," she had said. He was a Frenchman.

He had, his father supposed, a title?

Oh, no indeed. He was a man of letters. He was writing a book on (someone of whom David had never heard) Edgar Allan Poe, and he was here to get (this had a sinister sound to David) some very important information on the subject.

Oh, then he supposed she'd met him at the Warings'. Another one of their Bohemians, he expected.

She didn't know what he meant by Bohemians. He was very much of a gentleman, he dressed extremely well, his hair was never long. He had a small pointed beard and was, she would say, very distinguished in appearance.

Bugaboo names, names he didn't like, Edgar Allan Poe, the Warings, Bohemians, a man—a tall man with a pointed beard. This was undoubtedly the gentleman who had kissed his mother underneath the lamp. And now she wanted to give a party for him.

His father inquired when she intended to give this interesting party.

She said at once, "A week from Friday," and she wanted him to write the invitations because his writing was so much better than hers.

It seemed to be agreed. His father laid down his napkin and pushing back his chair went round the table to kiss his mother before departing for the office.

And there he was, left with all these goblin names to think of, in connection with that other far more sinister name that had now become a threat to his home, his happiness, and his security.

He had listened warily to his parents' conversation and as there was no further reference to the names, the thoughts, that caused him such uneasiness, he began to think that he would hear no more about Louise Denis. He was on the alert, however, and knowing he had been invited to their dinner party, managed on that night to slip into the upper hall and peeking through the banisters observe the guests as they arrived. There was no one among them with a short, dark beard. And after considerable reflection, he came to the conclusion that Louise Denis was very likely not the gentleman who had kissed his mother underneath the lamp.

Consoled by this and having gone for months and months with no mention of the dreaded name until that Easter Sunday, he had almost but not quite forgotten his imagined fears.

The old gentleman, unable to sleep, got up and seated himself beside the window, regarding the skyscrapers, the towers, terraces and tenements, the streets and avenues, and all the lighted windows. He was thinking about the four generations who used to gather around the dinner table to celebrate the annual festivals. And especially about one particular anniversary, being, as he was, so exquisitely tuned to the memory of that occasion, the conjoined presence of those unique and fascinating personalities, their voices, gestures, conversation, so delightfully persuading him of his own identity—little David Hare sitting beside his mother in that familiar dining room.

How beautifully the table was decorated for Easter, the white, the yellow tulips, the daffodils and freesia, the amber wine glasses and goblets, the favorite dinner plates, and all the people seated in the places they had always occupied.

There, opposite him, and seated on his right, little Mr. Friedermann, who called him "der kleine mann" and asked him if he would like to hear "A Little Night Piece" after dinner, next to him, Blanche, and then the outrageous, the fascinating great-uncle Alexander, who called him Shakespeare in honor of his mother's fond belief that he would some day be a poet, turning over his plate to look at the hallmark on the back: "Crown Derby! Where'd you get it, Laura? Damned expensive stuff."

And next to him, the exclamatory poor relation, Cousin Lucy, with her flattery, her insatiable curiosity. Beside her, his father, carving the roast, opening the champagne. And on his right, Granny Winchester. Then Great-aunt Adelaide, who shrieked so loud because she was herself so deaf. Next to her, Lily, and next to Lily, Cousin Agatha, who used to lay her hand on his and say, "David loves beauty, don't you, darling?"

Everything was proceeding much as usual. Great-aunt Adelaide was shrieking apropos of nothing. "Wildering? Wildering? There was a time when nobody had ever heard of Wilderings."

"If you had lived, my dear," suggested Uncle Alex, "in Jerusalem at the time our Lord was crucified, you would not, I am certain, have ever heard of Jesus Christ."

His mother, with a look of disapproval, changed the subject and asked what he had heard from the other Hares in Paris.

"Never open their letters. Always in debt. What shall I do with 'em, Shakespeare?"

And then his bright little thought occuring suddenly, "Why not set the hounds on them, Uncle Alex?"

"Capital idea. I'll put it to use at once."

Basking in his uncle's approval, delighted with himself, he suddenly heard his cousin Lucy calling across the table, asking his mother if she had heard that Louise Denis was coming back from France. Mrs. Waring had told her. Wasn't it delightful? He would soon be joining us on Thursday afternoons.

So that was the reason why he'd never heard his name. He'd been away in France. Now he was coming home. What might not occur? Would his mother meet him at the Warings'? Must it begin again, the worry, the anxiety? He took no further interest in what was going on around the table and when the ice-cream shaped like an Easter bunny was brought in, he did not join in the usual surprise and admiration and did not even touch his portion of the rabbit's head. And even before they all got up and bowed as was their custom before they raised their glasses for the usual Easter toast, Uncle Alex was on his feet and raising his glass, shouted, "One word's as good as ten. Fire away—Amen."

There was no change in his expression. What he had heard had destroyed his love for laughter. He had had enough.

But there was no end to it. For later in the drawing room when his mother and little Mr. Friedermann were at the piano playing the Sixth Symphony and were approaching the thunderstorm, Cousin Lucy, sitting next to him on the sofa, was talking to his father and just as his mother, bending over the music rack, was signaling to him that the storm was over, the bugaboo words—Warings', Edgar Allan Poe . . . what was she saying? The clouds dissolved, the sun was out, again his mother, smiling, bowing; the birds were singing. He waited for the shepherd's pipes, while Cousin Lucy continued to talk about the return of Louise Denis.

The old gentleman did not get up. How strange it was coming back after so many years to return to those old memories of childhood. And how intense he found them.

That birthday party of Olivia's, how crucial in its consequences. Reliving it, the scenes, the fluctuations of his moods, indeed the whole enchanting, poignant little drama, trembling as it had, on the very brink of poetry, filled him with an ironic, an almost tender, regard for the wayward contingencies of life.

It was a long time since that Easter Sunday. The goblin anxieties had disappeared. Spring was passing into June. The departure for Dune's End and the long summer at the seashore was imminent. He was happy, full of joy and anticipation. They were on their way to Olivia's party, Blanche and Lily, Jackie and Louisa Ware, who had joined them, the little girls in their party dresses, and he and Jackie in their velvet suits, all carrying birthday presents for Olivia, a merry little company, his mother in their midst. They had never seen the inside of Olivia's house; they were excited, curious. What would it be like? Would it be very grand and splendid? What would they have to eat? Would they dance, would they play games, would her grandfather be there?

Occupied with these conjectures, he had not even seen him approach, till suddenly they all stopped short; a gentleman with a pointed beard had joined them. He bowed, he lifted his hat, and then taking his mother's hand, he raised it to his lips. They exchanged greetings, and after a few more words, he bowed again, and she had said to him, "Until Thursday at the Warings', then."

They were on their way. Hardly able to realize what had happened (it seemed more like a tableau than an actual encounter), he tried to adjust his mood to a realization of what had really occurred. His mother had taken up the conversation where they had left it. Would they, she wondered, have the usual tails to pin on the usual donkey, or would they offer some fine new surprise?

They were approaching Olivia's house. They were all mounting the steps. He saw the windows in the huge conservatory at which he'd stood and stared so often. He had no interest in Olivia's house or in the children's excitement. All he needed was to stay beside his mother; he did not want to leave her side.

The door was opened by a butler who bowed as though he was acquainted with his mother and ushered them into the great marble hall. The glittering splendor of Olivia's house, more palatial than he had imagined, with its marble hall, its marble stairway, fountains, marble statues, spacious vistas and all those palms and plants and flowers, footmen in splendid liveries, music, voices, laughter, little girls in party frocks and boys in velvet coats and trousers, opened up to his astonished gaze. For an awkward moment no one seemed aware of their arrival. But the butler appeared to be conducting them toward their little hostess, and as they followed him across the perilous floor, Olivia, the heroine of the park, this fabulous young princess, was discovered at the foot of the great stairway encompassed by a veritable forest of green palm trees, welcoming her little guests. Doing her best to appear unconscious of the magnificence that surrounded her, she extended her hand. "How kind of you to come," she said, attempting to put them at their ease. She was dressed in a white frock without a single ornament as though such simplicity could assure her friends that she was no richer than the rest of them. And here were her guests, companions of the park, arrayed as he had never seen them dressed before, in their very best attire—sashes, necklaces, hair ribbons, laced collars, patent-leather pumps and all of them abashed and awed and ill at ease among such splendors.

Looking about him he heard familiar music played as though in an unfamiliar language from behind the palms, the "Kleine Nachtmusik," vibrating, trembling on the air. Why should it make him feel so full of sadness and desolation? He watched Louisa awkwardly presenting her gift. "How sweet of you, Louisa, to remember it is my birthday," said Olivia. She took the present and laid it down among a pile of other gifts. "David," he heard his mother say, "aren't you going to give Olivia your present?" He put his hand into his pocket for the small box, but there, as though his hand had frozen round it, it remained, and Olivia, continuing her role of perfect hostess, said, "Don't bother, David. I've got lots of presents, give it to me later."

The "Little Night Piece" floating silvery and tremulous spread out, touched everything he saw with beauty, magic. That fountain splashing in the distance and those plants and flowers and that naked marble figure with the water dripping from her shoulders and his friends in the midst of all Olivia's grandeur stamping about the stately hall dressed as for a festival of joy. And all at once his sadness turned to yearning, to the need for something beautiful, desirable, just within his grasp, for was he not here in this splendid palace, was Olivia's party not opening up for him a world of beauty and delight? Still grasping the birthday present in his pocket, he saw that the party had begun in earnest. A spectral voice, issuing from he knew not where, bade them good afternoon, and looking up he saw Olivia's grandfather, portly, imposing, a white carnation in his buttonhole, come forward, shake his mother's hand and tell her gallantly how beautiful she looked as the voice that surely did not belong to the old gentleman con-

tinued weirdly, strangely, and from every quarter of the marble hall—"Happy birthday, Olivia. Good afternoon, Louisa
Ware. Is this Master Theodore Moss? Can this be Lily Willoughby?" And while the children, startled, bewildered, looked
around, craning their necks, Mr. Wildering held out his hand
to greet him, and his mother bidding him shake hands, he
attempted to disengage his frozen fingers from his small box
and extend his hand in the direction of his host. "Is this little
Edith Winston? Oh, how do you do, young Samuel de Peyster," and then addressing him directly, "And here is Master
David Hare." To whom was he speaking? Whose hand was
he shaking? Olivia's grandfather was surely shaking his! Here
was Olivia's mother approaching with a gentleman beside
her, tall, dressed in a long black cape that reached to the
floor. Louisa had begun to cry. "How do you do," the voice
went on, "Miss Anna Lincoln." The gentleman in the long
cape was introduced as someone who was here to give them
all surprises. He turned and bowed and while the uncanny
voice determined, it would seem, to greet all Olivia's friends,
continued calling out the roll, at the same time the black-
caped gentleman with a sweeping gesture brought out from
his cape a shining hat, passed it round for everyone to see
that it was empty, and taking it up and peering in, wonder of
wonders, pulled out a dozen rabbits! "How do you do, Anna
Budinot? Good afternoon, Julius Brown." Where had the
rabbits gone? What was he doing now? He had presented
Julius with a large silk handkerchief. "Take it," he said.
"Shake it out." Embarrassed but delighted to be thus involved
in magic, Julius took it, shook it out, and grinning foolishly,
returned it, whereupon the man in the black cape flung it
out, retrieved it, held it in his hand an instant, and then
flourishing it in the air, released a little flock of bright canaries. The astonishment was such that pandemonium set in.
The children screamed, ran after the canaries, began hunting

for the rabbits. The voice, coming from Lord knows what direction, attempted to call them back, but to no effect.

He had not joined the other children but still stood beside his mother, more aware each moment of his amazement, wonder at the scene in which he found himself. As the figures shifted and changed and blended with the laughter and the voices, new surprises became more beautifully astonishing than ever. The man in black joining with the children flung off his long cape and danced around them, pulling from sleeves and waistcoat, from his pockets, brightly colored banners, handkerchiefs, confetti, while weird voices coming from heaven knew where issued orders—"Catch it, Samuel de Peyster. Here's a handful, Blanche Willoughby." The children wild with pleasure shrieked and screamed and scrambled. All was happiness and excitement. He still stood beside his mother. And now again he heard the music, the quivering strings. Never had a moment seemed as beautiful as this. He plunged his hand into his pocket, took out a small white box, and gave it to Olivia. She received it with her usual politeness and asked him if he wanted her to open it. "Yes," he said, and added shyly that he hoped that she would like it. She opened it exclaiming, "David, it is lovely, a silver box for bonbons," and smiled on him as though bestowing grace upon a favorite subject.

Louisa Ware fell down; the man of magic picked her up and danced with her. All the children began to dance. Then Olivia, turning to him, asked him if he would like to dance with her. Bewildered, embarrassed, overjoyed, he led her out among the children and intoxicated by the music and the knowledge that the princess of this enchanted palace had invited him to dance with her, he tried his best to guide his little partner and following the rhythms of the music, to join the other children on the marble floor.

The man of magic disappeared. The music continued;

the children went on dancing. The canary birds flew overhead, and now and then a frightened rabbit scampered across the floor. A young man dressed in an extraordinary costume with short breeches and white stockings appeared and whispered something to Olivia. The music stopped; Olivia, disengaging his hand, invited them all to come to supper with her in the dining room. Preceeded by his hostess, they led the other children into the great palatial room. The table was magnificently spread with flowers, and candles, and many-colored favors, the places set for all the guests. The children looked about them and were presently running round the table looking for their names on all the place cards and instructing each other as to where they had been placed. "Here, Samuel, here's your seat." "Louisa, you're next to Theodore." He heard Olivia's grandfather: "Here, young man, you have the place of honor," and Olivia calling for him to come and sit beside her on her right. The party went on without restraint. The children were putting on the paper caps which they had found inside their favors; they were blowing horns and trumpets. The orchestra struck up a birthday serenade. Finally the birthday cake with its seven lighted candles was placed before Olivia. She rose and attempted to blow out the candles. Such pride, such happiness, he had never before experienced, to be chosen in the face of all the others as her special friend and favorite.

He had forgotten all about that encounter on Park Avenue. He wanted only that his mother could see and appreciate his pleasure, his importance, and when the party was all over and they were walking home, he could not stop telling her how Olivia liked him best of all her friends. Hadn't she been wonderful? Didn't she think her house was beautiful? He could in fact not stop thinking of Olivia and talking about her, trying to make his mother assure him that she liked him the best of all her friends.

But his mother did not appear interested. She was inattentive, very busy, giving orders, packing trunks; and to his astonishment he discovered they were leaving at once for the longed-for visit to Dune's End.

That was the place he'd loved, thought the old gentleman, the most of all places in the world. The freedom of it, loosed like a bird, to run, to fly right off into the air and the blue sky, with the waves breaking and the wind blowing the salt spray from their crests.

On their arrival he forgot everything but his joy at being with his mother at the beloved Dune's End once more. The weather for some weeks was fine, and then a day of storm, and after—a clear bright morning, the waves high, the tide low, and the hard reach of the sand slate blue beneath the sky.

His mother with her book and parasol had retreated to the dunes. He was on the beach alone. The smell of the salt spray and the incessant roaring of the breakers exhilarated him; he ran along the hard, wet sand, challenging them to come on. They approached, the spray blown back from their foaming crests. It seemed to him that one great wave, lifted to an enormous height, stood up before him, beautiful and terrible with the sands and shells and seaweeds visible through its transparent walls. Slowly, its white crest foaming, it hissed, it turned, and then obscuring all its green translucent chambers, crashed and thundered in his ears. Knowing his mother was up there on the dunes, a refuge from his fear, he was determined to stand his ground. The beauty, the sound, the fury, mounted in him; frenzied by fear and exultation, he ran along the beach.

At what moment he became aware that she was no longer alone, he could not have told. But the knowledge increased his determination not to run to her for protection, but to continue to challenge the long procession of approaching waves. And as he ran and shouted, as the terror grew, so also grew his fear of the figure beside her on the dunes. Always that one great breaker stood up before him—terrible and beautiful beyond endurance. He waited, watched it break. His terror grew, became maniacal. He shrieked; he went on shrieking, and then as though pursued by all the powers of darkness and destruction, his knees giving way beneath him, the tears streaming down his face and almost drowning in his sobs, he turned and ran up the slope of the beach onto the dunes and fell sobbing convulsively in his mother's lap.

She comforted him. "But, David my darling, what is it? Control yourself. I am here. Nothing is going to harm you."

She turned, and though he did not hear the words she spoke, he knew that she was speaking in a voice of stern command. Still comforted by her embrace and the warm protection of her arms, he was aware that the figure beside them had vanished from the dunes. He was alone with her and she was assuring him that there was nothing more to fear.

Miss WILLOUGHBY was glad when her friend Oliver Hecht, who frequently dined with her, departed earlier than usual. He was a stimulating companion and one of the many friends who helped to keep her mind alive and interested in the problems of the younger generations. But tonight she longed to retreat into her past, and in the inviolate privacy of her solitary bed, she made a strenuous effort to forget the incredible changes that had since the death of her cousin Laura and the outbreak of the First World War plunged us all into a chronic awareness of global dilemmas and catastrophes, which with the advent of the atom bomb had suddenly grown to cosmic proportions, involving us in the awful recognition that we had now become the reckless guardians of this miraculous planet, which we were preparing in the name of our parochial ambitions and rivalries to wantonly destroy.

Let her return tonight to the heartland of her soul, forget for a while the decades that had so drastically changed her outlook and her environment, and leaving her bereft of the old familial ties and associations, had made of her, she often thought, a new and unrecognizable Blanche Willoughby. For had not David, whom she had thought never to see again, returned to New York, and was she not to see him on Thursday afternoon? "David, David," she cried aloud, not so much desiring to embrace him, as to gather to herself once more those imperishable years of her childhood and youth and early womanhood.

She remembered with great happiness her spontaneous response to David's question: Had she forgiven him? Then, thinking of the approach of that dark angel with the lifted arm, the beckoning finger, and resting as she often did in some haunting image of the thought she was pursuing, she closed her eyes and listening to the rush and rumble of the traffic on Sixth Avenue and to the heavy snoring of Mrs. Drew in the adjacent room, she repeated to herself the closing lines of one of her favorite poems:

And, in the isolation of the sky,
At evening, casual flocks of pigeons make
Ambiguous undulations as they sink,
Downward to darkness, on extended wings.

She surrendered herself completely to her memories and meditations. Events and moods of childhood rushed upon her. Thinking constantly of David, and as she was of so much importance to him, of Olivia Wildering, who seemed to come to life again as vividly as though she were still the little girl who had been so conspicuous a personage in the park where she had first beheld her.

"Poor Olivia, poor Olivia," she said aloud, visualizing the little girl whom she had known so long ago. Olivia was, like all the people figuring in her childhood, a creature of the park, born of the park, of the memory of water splashing in the fountain, of the voices and the laughter of children, and the spring days when tiny buds and flowers were scattered on the walks and crushed beneath the children's feet. She was a very living part of childhood, of its rivalries and attractions, its convictions and sudden illuminations. For was she not aware, like all the other children, that she was an heiress, that her grandfather lived in the great house on the corner of Thirty-sixth Street, and did she not frequently arrive in a big victoria accompanied by the old gentleman, who deposited her together with her governess and all her impressive paraphernalia at the northeast gate? How scrupulously she pretended not to act as though she were the most important personage among her little playmates. She could see her now, a rather handsome child with chestnut-colored hair and dark brown eyes and an expression of countenance a little strained, a little overanxious to play the part that had been imposed upon her. For she must not under any circumstances act as though she felt superior to the other children. On the contrary, she must make them feel that it was her privilege to have them for her companions. She must never boast; she must never assume lofty airs or act as though they were not in every way her equals. And feeling so strongly that none of them really were, how difficult it must have been for her to obey all these instructions without an air of condescension. It was at times quite obvious that she did not completely enjoy her beautiful obedience.

It must be confessed that her feeling toward Olivia had been, from the very first, suspicious. She did not think she really liked her, and it used to distress her to see that David was unduly pleased when she bestowed some particular favor on him. She always wanted him on her side when they chose the teams for prisoner's base but on the other hand she must admit to having felt a certain pride when she herself was selected as a special confidant. This sense that all the children seemed to have of wanting to be noticed by Olivia but at the same time not quite liking her was always somewhat disturbing. And there was that memorable day when Olivia suddenly became a heroine, after which she felt that she could hardly compete with her in David's estimation. Here, Miss Willoughby suppressed a gasp, remembering the horrendous scene.

For Mr. Pierson's bull had, the Lord knows how, escaped his tether and suddenly was seen stampeding across the park. Children shrieked and ran off in all directions. Nursemaids and governesses, forgetting their charges, ran screaming to a place of safety. Only Olivia held her ground; without a moment's hesitation she rushed to an abandoned baby carriage directly in the path of the advancing bull and placing herself squarely in front of it, challenged him to come on. And when two park attendants, appearing apparently from nowhere, shouting and throwing their coats from left to right, deftly turned him round and led him back to his accustomed haunt, Olivia had taken her singular act of courage very much for granted, as though to suggest that, under the circumstances, anyone would have behaved exactly as she had.

David was full of admiration, and it was then for the first time that she found herself in the unhappy position of attempting to hide from him her growing jealousy. But it was not until Olivia's birthday party when she watched him completely succumb to the spell of her glamorous surroundings that her suffering became acute. She had been unable to understand that all those flunkies and rabbits and canary birds, the noble proportions of the great house together with the enchantment of the music and the dance had for the first time profoundly stirred the deep wells of poetry that lay within his heart. She could not recover from the fact that Olivia had singled him out from all the others and made him so conspicuously her favorite.

It made her very miserable the following summer, when she was spending a month at Dune's End with her cousin Laura, that he constantly talked to her about Olivia. Had she noticed how she had made him dance with her and sit upon her right? In what an unhappy position she found herself. Anxious not to display her feelings, she would do so, suddenly, angrily, humiliated by David's accusations of her jealousy. Did she think, he would persist, that when he returned to New York, Olivia would continue to like him so much or would she have forgotten?

Olivia had not forgotten, and when they returned to New York and all the children were again assembled in the park, it was very plain to everyone that she had chosen David as her favorite friend. She did nothing to disguise her admiration for him and took it quite for granted that he was at her beck and call. Presently a legend grew up about them. They were the little sweethearts of the park. And so for years she had to watch the idol of her heart calmly appropriated by this self-assured and condescending girl. By the time she came out, she had chosen for herself the young man she fully intended to marry. He sent her flowers; he danced cotillions with her; he went through all the gestures of devotion.

Watching all this with a jealous and observing eye and long before he came to her for counsel and advice, she was fully aware that he had been trapped into playing a false not to say an intolerable role. And when he finally admitted that he was bored, sick to death of her—she had no ideas, only opinions stubbornly held and constantly repeated, with all of which she firmly believed that he agreed—she was surprised at her own delight and satisfaction. He begged for her advice. Did she think that he could honorably withdraw and leave the field free for other suitors?

What a joy it was to be his confidant. He was now at Harvard and it was easier for him to free himself from his entanglement than if he had been living in New York. These were the years when she was not only deeply in love with him but felt herself to be the keeper of his heart and soul.

Old Miss Willoughby, reviving these memories, realized that the love she felt for David had been inseparable from her love, her positive adoration, of his mother. Being Laura's son, had he not seemed to her more to be worshipped and adored than any other child? Was he not a part of that great joy she used to feel when she awoke at Dune's End listening to the cry of gulls, the sound of waves breaking on the beach? Had not the very games they used to play together been an echo of the knowledge that he was Laura's son? And how could Olivia Wildering through all their childhood years pretend to such a right in him as she herself possessed?

She loved him tenderly, romantically. She knew little of passion (what young girl did, in her day and generation). How handsome he was, how charming. He had his mother's eyes. She adored him. He had taken her into his confidence. With her approbation he was freeing himself from Olivia's hold upon him. Had she not assisted in writing that momentous letter which had explained his desertion and neglect of her. He could no longer be made and molded by her ideas and opinions; he had his own and she must understand once and for all that he had no intention of allowing her to plot and plan his future life. He had no interest in banking and above all he was not going to be pushed into easy success by the magic of her grandfather's name. Olivia's behavior to her at this time was both touching and characteristic. Whenever they talked together of him, she assumed her old proprietary air and acted as though he belonged exclusively to her. It was all very difficult, and David's position, when he returned for vacations, was, to say the least, bewildering. Respecting Olivia's indomitable pride, he had allowed her a temporary victory.

David's college years were beset by many difficulties. He was in constant conflict with his father, who was eager for him to take an interest in his future career and criticized him severely. What was the meaning of all these snap courses he was taking—the History of Art, the Study of Aesthetics? What was that going to do for him? Was he giving him an expensive education for the purpose of turning him into a dilettante, a chatterer about pictures and painting and the love of poetry? It seemed that at this time there was no one beside herself to whom he turned for comfort and understanding. She shared his love of poetry, and it was at the time that they were reading Swinburne together that he found the name for her that she cherished still—"Sister Swallow." And now repeating the familiar lines

> Swallow, my sister, O Sister Swallow,
> How can thine heart be full of the Spring?

she felt again the sweet sensations like the passing of a swallow's wing across her heart.

Mrs. Drew had stopped snoring, and the sound of traffic on Sixth Avenue had diminished. She heard a clock strike twelve. Tomorrow she would have her tooth out. She must try to go to sleep. Her memories were escaping her. She grasped at them. Their sequence was disturbed. She could not let go of the old Blanche who used to sleep with David's letters underneath her pillow. She had been his confidant, his sister. He had never been in love with her. He had never really broken with Olivia. The years retreated and advanced. There had been the death of David's father. Lily had married. She had gone to live with Cousin Laura. David had graduated and returned to study law at Harvard. He was not so much in her confidence. He was attempting, now that his father was dead, to carry out his wishes. Letters had become less frequent. Did she try to hide her love from Laura? They had not spoken of it. They spoke of David constantly. Had he chosen the right profession? They had such hopes for his future.

Then there had been that unmentionable trouble into which they had all been plunged—the girl in Boston who claimed that David was the father of the child she was about to bear; all so secret, so carefully hushed up. When, after unspeakable distress and with Uncle Alexander's intervention and the assistance of his lawyer, the miserable girl's account of David's part in her dilemma had proved as false as it was foolish, he had emerged freed from either paternal or financial obligations but not without chagrin and loss of his self-confidence. Knowing she was aware of his part in the unsavory situation, he had ceased to make her his guide and confidant. It was for her an awkward and unhappy time, the more so as she saw that he was turning to Olivia, whose indestructible loyalty as well as her ignorance of his escapade had assisted him in regaining his self-respect.

She had not been at all surprised when a year before his graduation from the law school he had announced his engagement to Olivia. He was rather self-conscious when he talked with her about it and spoke of her firmness of character and of the respect he had for her integrity. She tried to act as though she had never listened to his earlier complaints of her and did her best to offer them both her warmest congratulations and the sincerest wishes for their future happiness. But it was not very long before she perceived that he was again beginning to be bored and irresolute. He put on, however, a very buoyant front, and it was plain enough to see that he was determined to carry out his plans.

And now before sleep overcame her, dragged her down into oblivion, she grasped, she clutched, she saw the well-remembered pageant, this little scene and that. Standing among the other bridesmaids, holding her bouquet of sweet peas tinted the color of her gown, she saw it all—Lily the maid of honor, and Jackie Ware David's best man, and the rector in his voluminous robe, and Olivia herself in white satin and old lace, complacent, triumphant, David acting his part with courage. David slipped the ring onto Olivia's finger.

She saw her cousin Laura in the front pew, lovely in a gray gown, with Uncle Alexander erect and unmistakably disgruntled. The ceremony was over, the Mendelssohn wedding march proclaimed triumphantly that Olivia and David were man and wife.

Thoughts of Cousin Laura filled her mind. She had risen from her knees. Escorted by Jackie Ware she followed the procession. She waited in the vestibule with Uncle Alex, who would accompany her to the house in his ancient landau. She would be late. But she herself must hurry with the other bridesmaids, leaving the lumbering carriage far behind.

So much haste and flurry, guests arriving, pushing, exotic perfumes, clatter of conversation, laughter, voices, conspicuous costumes, strains of orchestral music. (A flood of memories—Olivia receiving her little guests beneath the palms . . . the fountain . . . the marble figure.) Ascending the great stairway, she chatted, she laughed, her thoughts were all with Laura. The receiving line was forming in front of the large Renaissance fireplace. Mr. and Mrs. Wildering with David and Olivia stood awaiting Laura, whose delay had filled her heart with apprehension. Her own future, David's future seemed to wait on her arrival.

Finally, unruffled, apparently serene, she came, and placing Uncle Alex in her care and disregarding Olivia's reproachful glances, slipped into her place next to Mrs. Wildering. She bowed, she smiled, disguising the sorrow in her heart, acquiesced with all who came to shake her hand—"Oh, yes indeed, a lovely bride," "how fortunate he is," "a childhood love affair," "so romantic," "such a suitable alliance."

When the bridal feast was drawing to its close, she saw her again with the other guests crowding about the door to watch the final ceremonies. As David raised his glass to give a sudden toast, she saw her exchange a glance with Uncle Alex, who was standing at her side.

Is David sitting next to a little girl who cuts her birthday cake adorned with seven pink candles, or confronted with another cake of marvelous structure and dimensions; is he rising, lifting his glass amid the shouts and laughter of his ushers and the bridesmaids in their gowns of variegated hues?

> Here's to the olive that she picked
>   From the only olive tree
> That grows in Eden's groves replete
>   With fruits of all variety.
> She gave it to me in exchange
>   For an apple she will eat,
> Provided God will undertake
>   To drive from Eden the old snake
>   That threatens our felicity.

Laughter, applause, shouts of ushers, congratulations of bridesmaids. Floating, drifting, clutching at the memories, the pictures—Olivia in her wedding gown, David in his frock coat, the gorgeously appointed table—and thinking of Cousin Laura's smile, old Miss Willoughby drifted, sank, rose again. Great waves of sleep enveloped her.

M ISS WILLOUGHBY's tooth was out. She was seated in a taxi with Mrs. Drew beside her on her way to West Fourth Street, and she was in a state of great exhilaration. The extraction which she had dreaded so much was over, and she had not, as she had so idiotically thought was possible, died during the ordeal. Tomorrow she would see David, whom she had feared she would never see again. She was happy she had forgiven him. It seemed almost impossible for her to comprehend why she had never written him or why in all these many years she had had no word from him. The mysterious young woman who had ensnared him was dead. There had been a second great world war. The bones of little David, whom he had abandoned, had been bleaching at the bottom of the South Pacific Ocean for almost twenty years.

Mrs. Drew, who had been chattering at her side, about she knew not what, was telling her that now her tooth was out, she must rest in preparation for her visit from the boyfriend. Angered by the forbidden word, she had said, "How many times do I have to tell you not to use that absurd expression. He is not my boyfriend. I am an old woman, believe it or not, who has never had a boyfriend."

"Excuse me for living," replied the injured lady, lapsing into silence, which remained unbroken until they arrived at home. And though she was sorry she had hurt the garrulous creature, it was a great relief to find her so subdued that there was little conversation between them during lunch. And when she had said on leaving the table that she was going to make herself scarce for the rest of the afternoon, she settled herself with great satisfaction in a comfortable chair beside the window to read David's latest book, which she fully intended to finish before his arrival.

But she was unable to read because she was thinking of that afternoon a few days after David's wedding when she and Laura had lain together on the dunes. Her mood was so tuned to the scene and to their close communion, grieving as they were for David's loss and full of regrets that he had married Olivia Wildering, that it seemed to her that she was actually there.

She heard the screeching of the gulls and the sound of waves below them breaking on the sand. The breeze, warmed by the sun and freighted with the salt smell of the sea, blew over them. And suddenly she knew that Laura had broken the bonds of their communion and was pondering some secret of her own, and when she asked her if she had ever read the poems of Alice Meynell, she said with considerable bewilderment that she knew a few of them. Had she not written something about lambs or sheep?

"Yes," she had answered, "a lovely poem." But it was not of a "Shepherdess of Sheep" that she was thinking; it was of a sonnet which had been for many years, when she was a young woman, the under-music of her nights and days. And adding that it was not, she expected, a very great poem, she repeated the fourteen lines from beginning to end in her beautiful, perfectly cadenced voice:

"I must not think of thee; and, tired yet strong,
    I shun the love that lurks in all delight—
The love of thee—and in the blue heaven's height,

And in the dearest passage of a song.
Oh, just beyond the sweetest thoughts that throng
   This breast, the thought of thee waits hidden yet
     bright;
     But it must never, never come in sight;
I must stop short of thee the whole day long.
But when sleep comes to close each difficult day,
   When night gives pause to the long watch I keep,
And all my bonds I needs must loose apart,
   Must doff my will as raiment laid away,—
     With the first dream that comes with the first
     sleep
I run, I run, I am gather'd to thy heart."

Then while the waves continued to break, and the gulls shrieked, and the great white clouds above her cast their shadows on the dunes and the sunlight came and went, she revealed to her the intimate and poignant story of her childhood, the years that followed her debut, of her many suitors and the fact that she had never fallen in love with any of them, and how she had finally married Leonard Hare and of her consternation on their bridal night and later of the wonder and joy of looking at her little son and of the great content and happiness that she had experience in her early years of motherhood, and finally of her meeting Louis Denis and of the great, the irrevocable love, the passion for him that had overwhelmed her.

She had been a loving child with a great capacity for joy and a greater for affection of which she had received but little. Her mother, a very beautiful woman, loved and adored by everyone, had died when she was too young to inherit even the slightest memory of her. She did however have a faded photograph that she used to slip beneath her pillow every night and upon occasions lift to her lips and cover with

her tears and kisses. Her father, a gay and extravagant gentleman, more addicted to losing one fortune than capable of
building up another, was handsome and witty and a great
favorite with his friends. She adored him; his affection for her
was elaborate and decorative, but he enjoyed the company
of his boon companions more than that of his little girl and
did not spend much time in her society. He did, nonetheless,
manage to have someone to keep, as he expressed it, a moth-
erly eye on her and at the same time to manage his household.
These ladies were of various types and temperaments and
their tenure was never of long duration. It might be thought
that with all these lugubrious vicissitudes she would have resembled one of those little heroines of fiction, enjoying their
own sorrows and perpetually drenched in tears, who were so
dear to children of her own generation. But quite the contrary
was the case, for she was filled with intelligence and curiosity.
Life provided her with many gratuitous delights, a sunny
morning, the perfume of a flower, the song of a bird, the enjoyment of her music lessons, so that at an early age she was
able to invent her own small philosophies and to discover her
capacity for joy as well as for heartache and disappointment,
and when at the age of fifteen her father was suddenly killed
in a railroad accident, she was able to sustain a change, not
only in her physical environment but still another of those
distressing changes in custody and guardianship, without too
serious a disturbance to her nervous equilibrium.

Her grandmother, a somewhat formidable old lady, who
lived alone and enjoyed freedom from responsibilities, had,
to everyone's surprise, offered her a home and considerable
assistance in finishing her education. Her house on Twenty-
third Street had character, created moods and climates of the
heart. The high-ceilinged, well-proportioned rooms conveyed
a melancholy elegance; the ancestors on the walls, in spite of
their imposing presences and courtly costumes, had lost their

luster—their frames needed regilding, and the canvases on which they were depicted were ingrained with the dust of many years. There were stains on the wallpaper, and the beautiful carpets were worn and faded, the furniture was of the same period as that of the ancestors; there were many authentic pieces, but the elegant chairs and sofas sadly needed upholstering, and the mahogany had received so little attention that it had long since lost its grain and gloss; the parlor shades were generally lowered, and the walls exuded a chill odor of mold. She was homesick, she missed her father and felt the ache of old associations. She could not for some time feel anything but awe for her formidable grandmother. She moved about the house and responded to its moods; she wondered how long it would remain her home.

Mrs. Winchester, who because of a long-existing quarrel with her son, had seen but little of her grandchild, observed her carefully; the girl she decided had quality what with her beauty and her talents and that something she could not quite define, she had the makings of a great lady. She resolved to do her best to make her one. She must have a better music-master—her voice and her playing of the piano were excellent; she must learn to be fluent in French and above all to have the proper companions; she would choose a good school for her, and when she was the proper age, she would bring her into society. And when, after her debut, she became the belle and beauty of the season, her grandmother was not at all surprised.

She had no lack of suitors. She enjoyed their admiration and companionship, but when she had danced her way, and at her grandmother's expense, through several seasons, she had chosen none of them, she began to feel that there was something wrong with her—she could not fall in love. She had heard so much among her friends about the agonies and joys of this condition, but had never herself experienced any of these agitating emotions. Getting married should certainly have been her business; this was plain enough to see, for her grandmother's straitened circumstances had been sorely taxed by her dependence upon her. "Poor old Granny" had done her best to give her every opportunity to make a rich and suitable marriage—dipping into her principal to give her a proper chance. The time had come when she must make a choice among her suitors. About matrimony she had had the most romantic ideas—there should be a beautiful, an almost mystical communion—a meeting of souls—and as it seemed to her more than unlikely that she would ever find such a communion, why should she wait on the improbable? She would choose among these young men, who told her that they loved her and wished to marry her, the husband of her grandmother's selection.

Leonard Hare was rich, he was well-born, he had an excellent position in the great Wildering banking house, and it was rumored that some day he might become a partner and, moreover, she genuinely liked him. He had repeatedly told her that he would commit suicide or remain a bachelor or do something equally absurd if she would not be his wife. He had, except for the impossible requirement, everything to recommend him; he was handsome, he had a warm and generous nature, he had quite humbly adored her for three years. How nice it would be to have a home of her own, to be able to entertain her friends, to give her grandmother a sense that she was always welcome in Leonard's pleasant house on Park Avenue. So after much deliberation, the old house on Twenty-third Street was made ready for the great event; chairs and sofas were reupholstered, tables and cabinets reconditioned, the bloom and color restored to fine old carpets, and the family portraits given back their striking personalities and costumes.

On the night before her wedding, her grandmother had

said she wanted to have a little talk with her. She wished her
dear mother were alive to say to her what she felt it was now
her duty to convey. Then, much embarrassed, she went on to
tell her that she was entering into the state of matrimony, and
if she should feel surprised at the demands that Mr. Hare
was sure to make upon her, she must always remember that
he was a perfect gentleman; these demands (or had she said
these pleasures) of the marriage bed were an important, a
very natural part of matrimony.

When returning the next day with Leonard from Saint
George's Church, she stood up beside her grandmother to
receive compliments and congratulations, she felt as she
looked about her that this extravagant outlay of capital on the
part of her old grandmother expressed more than a grim resolve to do her best by her, but was an eloquent expression of
her love. She wanted before she left this house forever to let
herself go and tell her how deeply grateful she was for her
love, for all her wise and carefully thought-out plans, in fact
for everything. But what with one thing and another, festivi-
ties and the bridal breakfast and having to get into her traveling clothes in such a hurry, and time only for a brief and self-
controlled embrace (for Granny was not one to indulge in
public display of private feelings), she had no chance to tell
her what she longed to say. And the last glimpse she had of
the formidable old lady was seeing her among others on the
sidewalk, throw a handful of rice after the departing carriage.
And off they drove together in Uncle Alex's lumbering landau
(the very same in which she had later gone with him to
David's wedding). He had loaned them his house in Ardsley,
the "family rookery," he called it, for their honeymoon.

The gulls still shrieked, the sound of the waves was incessant. The air was cooler now, the wind was not so strong. It
was a long drive, Laura's voice continued. She was terribly
fatigued. Leonard was in exuberant spirits and kept telling

her what a lucky man he was and how desperately he loved
her. The afternoon was lovely, haymaking was in progress, and
the air was sweet with the smell of hay and sunshine and the
fragrance of pollen. Great white clouds were in the sky.
Leonard kept trying to recapture and keep her hand in his. She
kept thinking how beautiful the world was and started
to repeat to herself to the rhythm of the horses' hoofs and
the rumble of the carriage wheels a monotonous refrain which
went on and on for hours, "a summer afternoon, a summer
afternoon." They talked of many things—the ceremony at the
church, the reception at the house, Uncle Alexander and the
house that he had loaned them, a fine place, Leonard said;
it had been in the family for several generations. She had
made a conquest of his old uncle. She must be careful not to
compete with his other relatives for a big slice of his will; they
were always jockeying for position in his good graces. He had
so many relatives and all she possessed were those portraits
and her poor old Granny. She was in a kind of trance and
hypnotized by that refrain, "a summer afternoon, a summer
afternoon." And so they went on from one subject to the
next, and presently the sun went down behind the horizon,
twilight shortened, stars came out, lights appeared in scattered
houses. On they drove. The night was warm and dark around
them. At last, they left the high road, turned into a long
avenue and drew up in front of Uncle Alex's rookery.

The house was brightly lighted and Mrs. Riley, Uncle
Alex's housekeeper, was at the door to greet them. A late
supper awaited them. The table was festively set and the wine
and food delicious. She was not hungry but Leonard's appetite
was fine; he complimented Mrs. Riley on her cooking and
helped himself plentifully to Uncle Alexander's claret. She
watched him eat and drink and wished that they could stay
as long as possible at supper. Would there be dessert? Would
they drink their coffee in the other room? When coffee had

been served, Leonard put down his napkin, rose, and drew back her chair. They tarried a while in the parlor and here again, she wished to linger longer. If only there were cigars that she could offer him to draw out their conversation. But here, alas, was Mrs. Riley interrupting. Should she close up or would they do so themselves? Leonard looked at his watch and said, "By all means, Mrs. Riley, it is time for you to lock up and we will go to bed."

The bedroom was cool and fragrant. The windows stood wide open to the night. There was a lamp on the table near the high four-poster bed, which was opened with her night-gown carefully laid out. They had not known what to say to each other, where to look, or what move to make. Finally, Leonard broke the long embarrassed silence. He guessed, he said, they'd left his luggage somewhere else. He would leave her to undress and find it. And, adding that he would be back presently, he went into an adjoining room and shut the door behind him. She realized that when he returned, he would be ready for bed and expecting to find her already undressed and awaiting him.

She undressed in a great hurry, slipped on her nightgown, and deliberating a moment, left the bed and crossed the room to one of the large, wide-open windows. There was no moon. She thought that she had never seen the sky so full of stars, or known a night so still. She longed to escape. Listening, she heard a lamb lost in that wide universe of stars, bleating for-lornly. "Little lamb, who made thee, Dost thou know who made thee?" Blake's tender question seemed to amplify the silence—she found that she was weeping uncontrollably.

She was not aware that Leonard had come in, crossed the room, and was, in fact, beside her. And when he bent, lifted her in his arms, and carrying her, unprotesting, to the bed, laid her gently down upon it, her astonishment was not so great as her alarm. And, when caressing her and whispering words of love and adoration, he unbuttoned and slipped off her long, white nightgown, she did not—in fact, she was unable—to protest. She simply lay there shocked, humiliated by her nakedness, and even when he turned, put out the lamp, and hurriedly divesting himself of his nightshirt, climbed into bed and took her in his arms, she was still unable to protest.

That the gratification of physical desire should be the natural, indeed, the beautiful consummation of love was a thought she had never entertained. Completely innocent and uninformed, she thought of what her grandmother had told her the night before her marriage, that she must always remember that Mr. Hare was a gentleman. She must consent to the demands he made upon her. They were natural and to be expected. How shocking, how unexpected they were, but she was determined, nonetheless, to conceal from Leonard her unwillingness and her chagrin. She was his wife and not to yield to him would surely have been a breach of those solemn promises that she had made. And so, passive and without protest, she endured the initiations of her marriage bed. Later, she lay in his arms, listening to his words of love, the tender assurances of devotion and fidelity, raised above the level of his passion. And when at last, his lips against her cheek and still continuing to tell her how he loved her, he fell fast asleep, she loosed herself from his embrace and lay long awake, telling herself she was his wife—the woman he possessed.

When they returned to New York after the honeymoon, she was happily occupied rearranging the house on Park Avenue, lending it some of the grace and charm of her own personality. How wonderful to have a home of her own and to find her role in society had been greatly changed—she was now a married woman, she was the charming Mrs. Hare, as she often heard herself called—the most beautiful young matron in the neighborhood. She felt for the first time a sense of real security, what with Leonard continuing to be so proud of her, so devoted and later building her that pleasant house where she could spend her summers near the ocean.

And finally that wonderful moment when, filled with joy that she knew she would not again experience, she laid her eyes upon her little son! What a marvel he was, finished to absolute perfection, the tiny fingernails, the small pink feet with their accompaniment of toes and tiny nails, the eyes— the fringe of lashes and above, the eyebrows, definitely marked and arched, the well-shaped head, covered—she could hardly believe it—with a crop of dark brown hair. She had been allowed to take him in her arms—her child, her first born! Suddenly, endowed with the supreme gift of mother-hood, she felt that the duplicity with which she had fulfilled her wifely obligations had been more than amply paid for.

Every step in his development had brought her joy, and when she found that he could share with her the pleasures that had always been closest to her heart, what delight she took in his companionship! From an early age his capacity for wonder seemed to her astonishing. He had a way, very en-dearing to her, of lowering his voice in the presence of the major mysteries—the wings of a butterfly, a starry night, a shell discovered on the beach. She used to say, to Leonard's great amusement, "David has the soul of a poet, his response to nature is so direct—poetical," and how he had come to share with her the little human comedies that play so large a part in day-to-day existence, she was at a loss to know. There were secret bonds between them, affiliations. Life had brought her happiness, fulfillment; she was contented with her lot.

The voice had ceased. And suddenly, watching the dip-ping of the gulls and the spray blown off the crests of the advancing waves, she thought of David and of his marriage and of Laura's loss and desolation. "What is contentment," Laura finally asked, "a grateful acceptance of life, no perturbation or excitement, no agony or despair or ecstasy?" For it was in this condition of heart, she went on, that she had entered Mrs. Waring's drawing room on that late October afternoon.

The room was more than usually full. Tea had already been served, and several rows of chairs were drawn up in a semicircle around the piano. Little Mr. Friedermann was seating himself and a young violinist was already beside him, moving his instrument into position underneath his chin. Someone offered her a chair a little to one side, and she had no sooner slipped into it than the opening notes of the *Kreutzer* Sonata greeted her as though to say, "Come, this is exactly what you were waiting to receive." She closed her eyes and listened, and as she did so, it seemed to her that something— could it be a bird, she wondered—had escaped its customary prison and was free. Springing upward it soared, ascended, waited on the very brink of heaven, paused, again began ascending, soaring, aspiring, waiting. Upward it sprang and the winged phrase soaring, rising, stopping just short of heaven, repeated itself with ecstatic continuity within her heart.

She did not open her eyes until not only the sonata but the applause was over, and when she did so, trying to shake herself free of the spell the music had cast upon her, she looked up to see an unknown gentleman who was, with no further introduction than the knowledge of her name, speaking to her in an unmistakably foreign accent. He would ask for no apologies, he said, because it was through her face that he had listened to the music these remarkable musicians had just performed. Every note had been recorded in her countenance. Surprised, not knowing what to say, she had a curious sense of pleasure in the fact that they had somehow, and most mysteriously, shared the beautiful sonata together. Finally she said, "How strange," and then without embarrassment, "and how delightful."

And just as they were about to engage in further con-versation, there was Cousin Lucy gushing over the marvelous new violinist—and hadn't her husband positively outdone himself in his accompaniment. Cousin Lucy, it appeared, was acquainted with Mr. Denis, and she was presently giving him a long list of her perfections and accomplishments, when Mrs. Waring appeared and bore him away.

All during the week that followed, she was conscious of emotions suppressed but demanding investigation. What had occurred to her; what had that intrusive stranger—and without the permission of an introduction—claimed the right to vio-late; as one who had already shared its solitary movements, the privacy of her own soul? And why, having admitted the strangeness of sharing these secrecies, should she have de-clared her own delight in such a miracle? She was curiously exhilarated and felt an excitement it was impossible to repress. She would not, she resolved, go for some time to the War-ings'. In this case she would in all probability never meet the disturbing intruder again.

However, when the next Thursday came around, in spite of her resolve to stay away, she arrived at a very early hour at the Warings'—and sure enough there he was. Her pleasure at seeing him was undisguised. There seemed to be a natural-ness about their meeting, and the ease with which they talked together was surprising, and so, on the following Thursday and on the next, they met as usual. Certain facts about their life were soon established—that she was married, that she had a child, and that he was a bachelor, that his mother was an Englishwoman, and that he had gone to school in Eng-land. But after her death he had returned with his father to live in Paris, where he had finished his education and was now embarked upon a literary career. He was an alien in her own circle of acquaintances, but that there existed between them a mysterious affinity it was impossible for either one or the other to deny. It declared itself in a thousand subtle ways; in tones of voices, glances exchanged, acknowledgment of mutual understanding and of a mounting, ever-increasing happiness in the sheer delight each discovered in the other's presence. She could talk to him without it seeming strained or artificial about subjects she had always reserved for private speculation. Sometimes they escaped the Warings' early. They walked together in sections of the city where she was unlikely to meet anyone she knew. They had tea in out-of-the-way hotels and restaurants. Clandestine meetings, completely hidden from her husband or from the knowledge of anyone beside herself, had become an almost necessary habit.

Before she admitted to herself that she was, and for the first time, passionately and irrevocably in love, she began to think of ways and means whereby she could—and still possessing her new happiness—make it less secretive, less clandestine. Might he not come at her invitation to dine at Park Avenue? Might he not be admitted to the circle of her friends? And so, on an evening in March, when at his insistence, he was walking with her in the direction of Park Avenue, she burst out suddenly and with disquieting intensity declaring that it was time he became acquainted with her husband, with her friends. These secret meetings were intolerable. Their friendship should be openly acknowledged. There was no reason in the world to keep it secret. Aware that everything she said was not only awkward and untimely but basically untruthful, she went on to tell him she had made up her mind to invite him to a small dinner in the following week, which would, she added with complete ingenuousness, put everything on a different basis. Having arrived at Park Avenue, they stopped beneath the lamp just opposite her house. "Well," he demanded, and she knew his voice expressed complete and utter disbelief in all she'd said, "What next?"

And then, before she had a chance to answer, he had

stooped and kissed her passionately. Startled, profoundly agitated, and making no attempt to answer, she turned and hurrying across the street continued running until she reached her own front door.

And it seemed to the young Blanche, lying there in that great amphitheater of sea and sky and salt-drenched wind, that Laura's story was no secret to her—seeing before her, as she listened, a gentleman with a dark beard suddenly appearing on their way to Olivia's birthday party and hearing David, while they dug their wells down there on the sands below her, bid her cross her heart and hope to die, while he revealed the awful secret of that mysterious man who had come to take his mother from him, standing right here on these same dunes, where now she waited for her dear Laura to continue with the story of her love.

She had ordered the carriage and was dressed to go out. She stood beside her desk with a note in her hand, which she was reading and not for the first time by any means. "Mr. Louis Denis declines the kind invitation of Mr. and Mrs. Leonard Hare to dine with them on the twentieth of March" —just as formal and unadorned as that. He had declined her invitation and was determined not to enter into the circle of her family life but to keep their intimacy secret and clandestine. He had offered her a chance to end it once for all. She would give up going to the Warings' while he remained in town. "So be it," she said, and going to the dressing table, drew on her gloves. Why did her face not reflect the distress of her decision? It seemed alive with expectation and excitement.

Leaving the room, she descended the stairs, telling herself that she would call David to get on his things. She would take him off with her to do some shopping. He was waiting for her at the foot of the stairs and asked where she was going, pleading to go with her. "No, darling," she said. "It's late and

I have calls to make. I'll take you with me tomorrow afternoon." "Promise," he said. "Yes," she promised. He opened the door to let her out.

The carriage was waiting at the curb. Much to her surprise she told the coachman as she opened the door and got into the brougham, "To the Warings', Joseph," and no sooner was she seated than she began reviling herself. She had not seen him since the evening they had parted beneath the lamp. Had she been surprised at his rejection of the invitation? And had it not been tantamount to saying, we meet on the old terms or not at all? She reached for the little instrument that hung at her side, put it to her mouth and ordered the coachman not to go to the Warings' but instead to drive around the park and take her afterward to call on Mrs. Wentworth. As they turned into Fifth Avenue she closed her eyes. Her drive around the park would stiffen her resolution not to yield to her desire to see him once again. Up Fifth Avenue and into the park. Up the right side, down the left. This was the moment once and for all to put an end to their relationship, the opportunity he had given her, she kept repeating to herself. If she could resist her desire to see him today, she would have passed the worst of this terrific crisis in her life. Out at Fifty-ninth Street. And now armed against temptation and headed east in the direction of the Wentworths', overmastered by desire she seized the little instrument, telling Joseph she had changed her mind, would he turn and take her to the Warings'. The decision now irrevocable, feeling lost and irresponsible, she kept repeating, "Thank God, I will see him, he will be there." And when the carriage stopped, dazed and excited she got out and told the coachman he need not wait for her.

The drawing room was full, and all the people in it appeared to her like figures in a dream. She bowed; she smiled; cousin Lucy came to greet her. Mr. Friedermann took both her hands in his and said, "Meine liebe Laura." She was, she assured herself, conversing with a gentleman whose name was Mr. Monson. Yes, she said, she would like some tea. Managing somehow to keep these amenities in motion, there was a single presence of whom she was acutely aware. And the only conscious conversation she exchanged was carried on in silence between herself and Louis Denis, whom she saw halfway across the room conversing with a lady dressed in black. Through the buzz of talk and laughter and all that unrelated clack and clatter, she could hear him say that he had known she'd come, that his triumph was in short complete, and she, acknowledging his triumph, was nonetheless pleading with him, begging for mercy. Could he not ignore her presence, allow her to escape without a greeting or a word? Mrs. Waring was approaching, she was so happy to see her, she was not too late, for she had this afternoon a great surprise in store for all her guests. She had secured a cellist and our pianist, our dear friend, she laid her hand on Mr. Friedermann's arm. He was approaching—and in the face of all these people, she must greet him coolly like a mere acquaintance. Mr. Monson had arrived with the tea. He offered it to her. She turned and took it from him, aware her hand was shaking. No, she didn't care for cream or lemon.

Then offering her left hand to Louis Denis, she watched him take it, bend over it, and kiss the back of her white glove. What transpired next she would hardly be able to say. Had she drunk her tea? Had she refused the sandwiches that somebody had offered? Had there been general conversation? Was Mrs. Waring doing her best to bring her guests to order? Had the cellist seated himself? Was Mr. Friedermann at the piano? How was it that she and Louis Denis, while all the other guests were seated, had withdrawn and were standing near the doorway, and what was it they were about to do? "Come," he said, "before the music starts."

They had escaped. They were on the sidewalk. It was raining. Speechless, they walked together in the direction of Eighth Avenue. He took her arm and guided her across the street. To her relief, she heard a hansom clattering up beside them. It stopped. The doors parted. Bidding him a frantic good-bye, she clambered in, and he, with a hasty order to the driver, climbed in and sat down beside her. The doors were closed, and they were rumbling northward in their little cushioned box. Where were they going? What had she done to bring about so dangerous a situation? He was talking quickly and incoherently. The words he spoke seemed to wrap themselves about her like flames. What authority had he to talk to her as though he were her lover? It was raining in earnest. Frightened, and pulling herself together, she asked where they were going. "Oh, anywhere," he said. Anywhere, so long as she was here beside him and was free to tell him that she loved him. He had taken possession of her hand and was covering it with kisses. Where would it end, this awful illicit love that was consuming her? She prayed for sanity. She was not free, she said, to tell him that she loved him. Her freedom lay in asking him to let her make a choice. A choice, he asked contemptuously, between a husband whom she did not love, for whom she'd never had an ounce of passion, and her love for him? She drew her hand away and covering her face with both her hands, remembered her contented, unperturbed, and happy life at the center of which resided a love so tender, beautiful, and satisfying that it was impious of him to ask her to destroy it in succumbing to this sudden and bewildering passion. She stiffened herself against it. Were there no limits to his daring, to his assumption?

"You failed to mention," she said severely, "that the choice is not between my husband and yourself but between you and my little boy." "I can give you sons," he said, "whom you will love as much and more than this child born of a passionless marriage."

She took her hands from her face. "Never, never," she cried fiercely, ready now to fight for everything she had herself so recklessly endangered. Begging him for mercy, she said he must be generous to her. She asked him weakly, almost childishly, to take her home, to allow her to forget her madness, her insanity, and shrinking away from him as far as possible, wept without control. She looked out. They were crossing Fifty-ninth Street; they were almost at Fifth Avenue. What orders had he given to the driver, she demanded. He said he had told him to go north and get them to Fifth Avenue. "Oh, tell him now," she begged him weakly, "to take me home as soon as possible." She was sobbing like a child, repeating brokenly that she must beg him to forgive her. She must implore him to get her home.

To her surprise she heard him give the driver the correct address and sink back into his corner of the hansom. They were silent now. The pavement shone brightly in the rain, reflecting the carriage lamps that passed them as they rumbled down the avenue. She did not dare to speak. The sound of horses' hoofs on the pavement, rhythmic and accustomed, seemed somehow to assure her that life was not desire and expectation, insanity and madness, but contentment and security, that when she stopped at her own front door, stepped from the hansom and entered her own home, she would say good-bye forever to danger and desire and expectation and clasp her safety to her heart like some imperishable treasure.

But he was speaking now, not recklessly, not passionately, but soberly and calmly. He would, he said, allow her time to make a serious decision. He would leave and not return for several months but then, he warned her, he would come back and expect of her a considered and an honest answer, not to the demands that he was making of her but to the demands and necessities of her own heart. The confidence with which he spoke surprised her. She made no effort to contradict him or deny the claims he made upon her but sat in perfect silence listening to his declaration.

When the hansom stopped in front of her own house and the doors that closed them in were opened, he alighted and assisted her to the sidewalk. Incapable of speech, without so much as bidding him good-bye, she mounted the stoop and rang the bell. The hansom drove away. When the front door opened and she found herself inside, the only feeling she experienced was one of intense relief. "Thank God," she said, "thank God." She had escaped to home, to safety, to the familiar ways.

She had made the park her refuge, a place to which she brought her sorrow and her problems, struggling with desires she could not master and with a love that did not diminish but grew stronger as the days went by. Week followed week and spring was on the way. She had had no word from him. Could it be possible that he would not return? Why had he come into her life? She had moments of sudden anger. What was it he had to offer her, this impertinent intruder? How could he possibly believe that she would destroy the firm foundation of her content? She would put him out of her mind. She would forget that she had ever met him. She made a practice of condemning herself for every thought she had of him. But there had not been a moment in which her mind had not returned to hours they had spent together, and words that he had spoken to her had become a perpetual under-chorus to conversations that she carried on with others.

And listening, she suddenly realized that the anguish she revealed had been endured during that period in her own childhood when she had found in the radiance and beauty of this beloved woman all the happiness that she had ever known. The wind had died down, the clouds were heavy over the dunes, a gull skimming the waves flew up and plummeted into the sea as Laura concluded her long, uninterrupted story. And as she listened to her voice, it seemed to her assisted by those fragmentary memories of her childhood, that she had heard it all before. There had been that interruption of their progress on their way to Olivia's party—the appearance of the dark foreigner with the pointed beard, who had, to her astonishment, kissed her cousin's hand with such audacity and self-assurance.

Unprepared for him, the meeting and the greeting had been accomplished. And then when he had dropped her hand, she had, unchecked by caution and before she knew what she had done, said, "Until Thursday at the Warings, then." Beside herself, laughing and talking, she had gone on with the children to the Wilderings'. Later at the party, making decisions, planning frantically to leave New York before the appointed Thursday, and meanwhile responding to the lovely rhythms of that enchanting entertainment, mildly flirting with old Mr. Wildering, she had decided to write to Louis Denis, sending a letter in care of Mrs. Waring, stating her determination never to see him again—a dismissal, merciless, implacable, and utterly disregardful of the fact she had herself suggested they should meet.

There had been but little time to accomplish all that had to be done before her departure—packing, making arrangements for Leonard to be cared for, attending to a thousand domestic complications, but she managed to arrive accompanied by a joyful David on Thursday afternoon at Dune's End at just about the hour that Mrs. Waring's door was opening to receive her guests.

David's excitement at being once more at the seaside and his happiness in visiting all his favorite haunts swept her for a brief moment into the orbit of his delight. The past few months seemed unbelievable, but this—her summer here with David and a renewal of the joys they shared together—was reality. Indecision and anguish seemed to her a dream from which she had awakened. Had it not been something of a miracle that she had gone through all this agony alone and not a soul to guess what she had suffered?

All was well with her while she remained with David, but later when he was asleep and she herself had gone to bed, the momentary peace departed. The old intolerable ache returned with a redoubled anguish. An army of distressing thoughts assailed her. She died a thousand deaths each time she thought of the letter she had written Louis—dismissal, absolute and unrelenting. The more she thought of this, the more intense the yearning in her heart became. How long could she continue to endure it? She marveled at the discipline that she had practiced, the habit she had learned of subterfuge and silence. How had she managed this long-drawn-out deception, keeping her secret to herself and continuing her usual relationship to Leonard, yielding to his marital desires with the habitual compliance, lying in his arms and substituting as she lay there, oh, my God, what flights of her imagination, what ecstasies and pleasures unexperienced. How strange it was she thought that she could have lived so long without an inkling of her own capacity for giving and receiving passionate and requited love. And so, restless and unassuaged, her nights were passed, and in the first faint light of dawn, when the birds began to sing their small seraphic tunes accompanied by the constant sound of breaking waves, she would weep without restraint, making no effort to control her tears.

She lived from day to day dreading the weekends, when Leonard would usually come to visit them. Apparently he had no suspicion of the crisis through which she was passing. She had yielded to his sexual desires with neither protest nor enjoyment. He had never been adept at the art of making love. His demands upon her had now become direct and unemotional. As she lay beside him in the large cool room filled with the fragrance of the garden and the reverberation of the waves, she pondered her own plight and wondered how long she would be able to endure it.

She waited, hoping for some lessening of her heartache. She had, though she attempted to hide this from herself, expected some communication from him. He might have, through Cousin Lucy or Mrs. Waring, discovered her address, he could have written, he might, she must not even conjure with the thought, have come to see her here to plead with her.

Old Miss Willoughby, remembering Laura's story and vaguely watching a funeral procession forming outside Our Lady of Pompeii, became for an instant a little girl digging wells with David on the hard, wet sand. She crossed her heart and hoped to die and saw, as he told his secret, a gentleman with a dark beard whom she so well recognized.

How strange, how uncanny, thought the old lady. Had she not known always this sad story Laura told the young Blanche, as they lay together there on the dunes where he had come to plead with Laura many, many years ago?

THE OLD GENTLEMAN, who was visiting the Frick Museum, lingered in front of a portrait by Goya of an adolescent girl. He had returned to it for the third time not only because he was writing a book on Goya and the portrait interested him as a fine specimen of his work, but because it had stirred a memory in him that he was not able to shake off. What a portraitist he was! How well he understood the human family, those courtiers and courtesans and royal highnesses displaying with an almost sly delight in doing so, their vices and vanities and coy corruptions! And yet with what tenderness he could treat the young, the uncorrupted. What a luminous gravity suffused the face of this adolescent girl. One sensed in her an infinite but still unrecognized capacity for love and suffering. Tears filled his eyes. How he would have liked a daughter just like that, he thought, remembering that morning on the hillside amid the laurels and the evergreens.

Leaving the museum, he decided to walk back to his hotel. (Had it been that portrait that had set him thinking of his honeymoon?) Since telephoning Blanche, he realized that he was now a prey to all his early memories. And what an incongruous business that wedding trip had been, making a secret of it all as Olivia had been determined to do, not telling him where they were going, such a simple rustic place, she knew that he would love. She had chosen it for him, and it must be a great surprise. First there had been the night at the Hotel Touraine in Boston, arriving late, the suite awaiting them, all that was necessary for their stay already unpacked. Olivia had brought no maid, and how in the devil, he had wondered, had all this been accomplished?

Olivia, prepared to manage the situation, and efficient as usual, explained that there was an adjoining sitting room and that the bathroom would be at his disposal as soon as she could have a moment to wash up. In the sitting room he saw his pajamas and his dressing gown conspicuously displayed on the sofa. He heard Olivia in the bathroom. Presently she called to say that she was through. "Phew," he muttered, peeking through the open door as though expecting to see the Gold Dust twins concealed behind the bathtub. He undressed at a leisurely pace, and finally arrayed in his pajamas, lighted a cigarette—never had he needed one so much.

Going to the window, he pulled it up and leaning over the sill looked out into Tremont Street. Good old Boston, he thought, sniffing the east wind and the strong smell of the sea and, suddenly overtaken by the memories of his college days, lived over, all in a few moments, his sorry entanglement with Susy Green. Poor Susy—trying to hang that little bastard round his neck.

What a grim joke life was playing on him now. Olivia was calling him. "David, what *are* you doing? It's very late and I am dreadfully tired." He flicked his cigarette into Tremont Street and turned. God, if he could only take her in his arms and kiss her lips, her breasts, her hair, as he had once embraced that wretched little Susy. But if she were now to beg him to allow her to cling to her virginity for the remainder of her days, there was no favor he would have granted her with greater willingness.

He found her already in her narrow bed, arrayed in a very

appropriate nightgown, not too conspicuously low but beautifully flounced and ruffled at the neck and sleeves. Her hair was loose and shone around her face like a halo. He had rarely seen her looking prettier. He sat down on the bed next to hers, kicked off his slippers, and flinging his dressing gown aside, slipped in between the clean white sheets. Leaning toward him, she took his hand and held it firmly.

"David," she said, "I am so glad that we are married. I am sure that we are going to be happy."

"Yes," he answered, returning her pressure, "of course we are, Olivia."

"You know," she went on, after a moment of silence, "there was just one thing about the wedding I thought was not quite perfect."

"What was that?" he asked.

"I think your mother should have arrived in proper time to greet the other guests. Couldn't she have managed to persuade your Uncle Alexander not to take her in that ridiculous landau?"

"You don't know Uncle Alex. As easy to command the earth to stop revolving round the sun, as to get him to change his mind about a plan already made."

"Well, I didn't want anything to mar the memory of a perfect wedding day. Tell me something more about your Uncle Alex. Why does he still persist in driving around in that ancient landau?"

"He's an eccentric old fellow. I couldn't have done without him in my childhood. I was always waiting to hear what outrageous remark he was about to make at the family festivals, with all those personalities seated around the table."

"Tell me about them," said Olivia. "Do I know all those personalities?"

"Well," he said, counting them up, "there was Granny

Winchester, whom you know well, and Great-great-aunt Adelaide, unfortunately demised, for she was often one of the star performers. Then there was Cousin Agatha, whom you also know, Cousin Lucy Friedermann and little Mr. Friedermann, sitting on my mother's right, Lily and Blanche of course, and little David, with whom you are already so well acquainted, and at the head of the table was my father exactly resembling a walrus, especially on those occasions when he found it necessary to reprimand his son."

"How absurd you are, David! Your father didn't at all resemble a walrus; he was a very handsome gentleman and much resembled you."

"That is true and you will notice when I am old enough to have a son of my own to reprimand, that I will also bear a striking resemblance to a walrus—you know the one in *Alice in Wonderland*, with the drooping moustache and the sad eyes."

"Dear David, you're too ridiculous." She kissed him drowsily. "And some night when I am not so tired," she hesitated, "I want you to tell me how," she hesitated again.

"To go about the business," he suggested, "of getting that little boy whom I shall have to discipline?" Again he looked at her and saw to his surprise that she had fallen fast asleep, still clinging to his hand.

Then it came back to him almost too poignantly to be endured—the extraordinary days that followed—that secret place that Olivia had with such enormous pride in her discovery chosen for their honeymoon retreat. How pleased she had been at his appreciation of it. How many times she had told him she had chosen it because she knew how much he loved nature and the simple life. How lovely it actually had been—the tiny village in the New Hampshire hills, a single row of houses facing the quiet stream and the hill of exquisite proportions on which the sheep and cows were pastured. And then her other great discovery—Miss Rebecca Barnacle's immaculate boarding house, the single suite the place provided—which had been reserved for them—the large, the sparsely furnished dining room over which Miss Rebecca Barnacle with her salty and indigenous speech presided, the few "refined and simple" lodgers as Olivia described them, her superb and unconscious condescension to them as she managed most successfully to deprive the table conversation of all freedom and spontaneity.

One perfect day was followed by another. The June weather was sunny and serene. There were walks of great beauty in the immediate vicinity, and sometimes for longer excursions Olivia hired a dilapidated buggy. But wherever they might be and whatever they were doing, he became more and more convinced of the sad fact that he had married an incorrigible bore. She appeared to be very happy and talked a great deal about their future life. She wanted to make it simple and uncomplicated, and considering the little house on Fifty-fourth Street which her grandfather had given her as a wedding present, this would be very easy to accomplish. They would have only a few servants and she wanted no ostentation. In fact, she was going to try her best to live in their new home much as he had lived before their marriage.

He remembered the morning on the upland pasture where they had gone to see the laurel which blossomed there in great abundance, masses and masses of it, foaming up like great white clouds among the pines and hemlocks. How beautiful it was; the aromatic smell of pines and hemlock brewed in the sun delighted him. And the hum and drone of bees among the blossoms increased in volume as he listened. He looked at the blue sky, the floating summer clouds, only half attentive to Olivia's conversation, and finally thinking of the virginal nights they had spent together in Miss Barnacle's large four-posted bed, remarked that if they ever had a little girl he would like to name her Laurel.

"Why Laurel?" she inquired. "You should call her Laura, in memory of your mother."

"Oh, I was thinking of this moment here among these laurels," he explained.

"Oh, yes of course, dear, what a wonderful idea," she answered, still going on about her plan to return to New York for a few days before they started, according to schedule, for Bar Harbor, where they had planned to spend the remainder of their honeymoon with Mr. Wildering.

But why did she find it necessary to be in New York, he inquired.

It was very important, she explained, to have the little house in perfect readiness when they finally returned to town. She must see that servants were installed and everything in running order awaiting them when they began their new life.

And could all this be accomplished in a few days? Would the servants be left alone while they were at Bar Harbor?

She could put everything into the hands of proper agencies. It was important to begin their life in the new house without disorder or complications.

Well, if she insisted, he conceded, but it would be awfully hot in town.

She could manage everything in a few days, leave it to her.

A hermit thrush, or was it a vireo, was singing in the woods. He opened his hand to feel the sunlight fill it up. Let her talk on, he thought, and looking at her, saw to his surprise that she had fallen asleep. Continuing to regard her, he said to himself that this was the place, the moment, amid all this beauty, while they were alone together, that he should take her in his arms, and whispering passionate words of love, rape her, ravish her. But even if he had the inclination to do so, how would she take such a sudden attack upon her chastity? She would, he felt quite certain of it, have been shocked out of her wits, horrified at his audacity.

The thrush continued to sing, and the incessant humming of the bees still seemed to have increased in volume. The sunlight grew heavier in his hand. And then to his surprise, Olivia awoke, stretched out her hand for him to take and asked him drowsily if their honeymoon had not been wonderful? She hoped that he had been as happy as she had been.

"Yes," he said, still listening to the thrush, he had been very happy. And there they lay stretched out on the warm earth that smelt of pine and hemlock needles. Presently they were both of them asleep.

When they awoke, it was time to return, so picking up their baskets, they started on their long descent to the inn, gathering armfuls of laurel to take to Miss Barnacle, with the decoration of her house in mind. They agreed that this had been the happiest day they had spent together since their marriage.

They assisted Miss Barnacle in arranging the billowing clusters of laurel in her long white dining room, where they were much admired by the other guests at supper. After supper they lingered in the garden and he wondered at Olivia's silence, and later when it was quite dark and all the stars were out, they went to bed.

Lying beside her he wondered at the strangeness of their situation. She herself had displayed no consciousness of this. There, disembodied as a pair of angels, they had lain together night after night. Of all predicaments, was this not quite the queerest for a young man on his honeymoon to find himself confronted with? The silence made no answer. Out on the hillside he heard the tinkling of the sheep bells, which had become the theme song of these curious virginal nights beside his bride. Was she waiting on him or did he wait on her?

She reached out to take his hand. "David," she whispered, "don't you think tonight, after our beautiful afternoon, would be the time for you to give me those instructions about . . . ?" she hesitated.

He turned and took her in his arms. Then slowly, deliberately, he bared her breasts and slipped his hand beneath them. Cautiously he explored her breasts and the firm, cool flesh below. He felt the rapid beating of her heart and the quick drawing in and out of her breath. Her lips were opening, then, passionately, impatiently, she pressed them on his, which opened to her kiss.

"David, I love you, I love you," she urged breathlessly. "Teach me to be your wife, the mother of our child."

Her genuine expression of passion had surprised him. She had had little need of his instructions. She had yielded to him completely, whispering to him that she was so happy that at last they were really married.

The room was filled with summer fragrance. From across the river he heard the occasional tinkling of the sheep bells on the hill. As she lay asleep beside him, she seemed so quiet, so compliant, but oh! how well he knew that he would perforce assume obedience to all the loyalties of mind and heart and body to which she would hold and bind him now.

OLD DAVID, unable to shake off his memories, made up his mind as he took his luncheon at the hotel to go in the afternoon to the new museum he had not yet visited, to look at the Picassos. The *Guernica* was there. Goya and Picasso—was there not an extraordinary similarity between the two, each recording his response to the human comedy with the same audacity and anger, tenderness or humor, as the case might be? To have had in one short life both these artists to contemplate, was, thought the old gentleman, to have lived through God knows how many centuries.

Pushing back his chair, he decided to take a moment's rest before starting out again. But no sooner was he in his room and on his back than he was once more overtaken by his past. Why had he been unable to stem this tide of memories that had rushed upon him with his knowledge that Blanche was still alive and waiting for him with her warm assurance of forgiveness? And why this need to investigate a past that he had so deliberately attempted to forget?

Had she not been preternaturally aware of all he had endured in adjustment to this mistaken marriage? And had this not caused in him perpetual irritation and impatience to show her that she had been wrong in all her calculations? How eager he had been to pretend both to her and to his mother that he was happy and thoroughly enjoyed Olivia's management not only of her household but of himself and all his future plans.

The "little house" in Fifty-fourth Street, as she called it, he had declared quite perfect, and although he was never able to accustom himself to so much attention to minute details of order and wished often to disarray the books, the cushions, the objets d'art, which must be placed in the exact relationship to this or that or some other piece of furniture or decoration, he never showed how ill at ease he felt. And in the midst of all this adaptation to her arrangements he found it ludicrous enough to hear her continually talk about reducing life to such simplicity and lack of ostentation. Whenever he went with Olivia to visit his mother, he was overtaken by homesickness and infinite regret for having left a home so congenial and comfortable. So accustomed, he used always to think as he looked at the books and magazines within easy reach and the piano opened with music on the rack ready for her to sit down and play at any time she cared to do so. Everything in fact inviting one upon returning to take up life where one had left it off.

It had been a big mistake to knuckle down so quickly to Olivia's authority, but somehow and against his better judgment he was forced into this situation. Knowing well that Blanche and his mother were fully aware of his difficulties in adjusting to her complacent management of him and his affairs, he was eager to make them believe he had made no mistake in marrying her, that his pride induced him to a deliberate pretense of being entirely satisfied and happy in his married life. They knew all about it and he knew they did. And all three of them doing their best to maintain the pretense, their relationship grew strained and most uncomfortable.

Olivia took great interest in his work at Peabody and Simon, and as the senior partner of the firm was a great friend of her grandfather's, managed to wrest from him various favors and concessions. She wanted him to have before settling down to "uninterrupted dedication to the law" a long summer of European travel, and with Mr. Peabody's consent, plans were already in the making for what she liked to call our "actual wedding trip."

They were to have a summer in Europe, and this she thought was most important. He was so devoted to art and beauty that he must have a chance to see the old cities and the galleries, for, who knows, it might be difficult later on to take so long a time from work. This must be unrevealed until the evening of that dinner party, which would resemble as much as possible those old family festivals of which she had heard so much; the same relatives invited and, she hoped, a repetition of the old familiar scenes—the humorous exhibitions of character, Uncle Alex to be of course the principal entertainer. On this particular night she intended to spring a great surprise on the assembled guests by the announcement of their projected trip to Europe. Everything had been rehearsed.

Old David, suppressing his somewhat dolorous laughter, recalled the details of poor Olivia's miscalculated attempt not only to be the perfect hostess but the wise and resourceful manager of his life. No one seemed at ease. A queer restraint, as though attempting to adjust to a somewhat artificial situation, was laid on everyone. Uncle Alexander was on Olivia's right and he, opposite Olivia, had his mother on his right. Little Mr. Friedermann, Blanche, Lily and her husband, Cousin Agatha, Cousin Lucy, and Granny Winchester completed the circle of her guests. The table was elegantly appointed, and a pair of ancient candelabra (a wedding present from one of Mr. Wildering's partners) threw a copious candlelight upon the damask cloth. The flowers furnished from the Wildering greenhouse had been arranged by the old gentleman's butler, who in spite of Olivia's determination to have no menservants at the little house had been borrowed to assist the two maids in waiting on the table. The china and the glass were beautiful, and he almost hoped by way of diversion that Uncle Alex would take up his plate to inspect the hallmark on its back. He was uncomfortably awaiting some nod or signal from Olivia as to when and how she was expecting him to agree with her and complement every effort she was making to advertise their perfect partnership in plans and marital adjustments.

Cousin Lucy was certainly behaving in character and doing more than her bit in bringing back the past. "Your little house," she had adopted the family phrase, "my dear Olivia, is be*au*-ti-ful. In such good taste, these ancient candelabra, everything you have, Olivia, you might say, is a museum piece."

Agatha murmured something about David's love for beauty. Blanche was silent and attentive, and beautiful Lily was apparently trying to outdo Cousin Lucy in her extravagant enthusiasm for everything. Uncle Alex seemed strangely decorous. Granny nodded her head delightedly.

Olivia called across the table, "We expect some music after dinner, Mrs. Hare."

"Ja, ja, 'Eine Kleine Nachtmusik,' meine liebe Laura," little Mr. Friedermann assented. "And afterward we play together our duet—the thunderstorm, the breaking clouds, the shepherd's pipes."

Olivia explained that she had just had the piano tuned for the occasion. Everything, he had thought, going extremely well, an actual revival of the past. Olivia had turned to Uncle Alex; she was questioning him earnestly. "Should David have chosen banking," she asked, "instead of law? His father had always," she reminded him, "been in favor of his going in for banking. Tell me," she pressed him, "do you think that he is making a mistake?"

All other conversation was suspended. Everyone appeared to have heard Olivia's question and to be awaiting the redoubtable uncle's reply.

"I think my dear young lady," he said, facing her squarely, "that the only mistake that he has made has been in marrying you."

It had seemed to him that everybody gasped. He tried to pull himself together. "Bravo, the old incorrigible uncle is himself again. Congratulations, Olivia, our dinner is a great success."

The tension broke, everybody laughed. But Olivia, determined to pursue the subject, turned to David, "Your father and my grandfather believed that you were born to be a banker."

"Yes," he replied, "and my mother firmly believed that I was born to be a poet."

"Banker, broker, lawyer, thief. It's all the same, dear boy," continued Uncle Alex. "Your Olivia needn't worry; Peabody and Simon are sure to make the grandson-in-law of Croesus a partner in their firm before he's thirty."

His mother, who, he was aware, agreed with everything the old uncle had said, gave him a withering glance. Then Lily, attempting to change the conversation from one foot to another, remarked with animation, "I hear, Olivia, that you and David are planning to go to Europe in the spring."

Olivia shot him a suspicious glance as though to say, "You've told our secret, David." And then inquired sharply, "How did you learn of this my dear?" And before receiving an answer, said, "I'd hoped no one had learned our news. I wanted to surprise everyone myself."

"A surprise indeed, Olivia," said his mother. "How can he manage such a long vacation?"

"I've managed it myself," Olivia replied, with more than her usual self-importance. And speaking directly to his mother, wondered why he had not been abroad. She thought it quite essential that he should have at least a glimpse of Europe before he was harnessed to his work at Peabody and Simon.

"How wonderful!" cried Cousin Lucy.

The secret plainly revealed, everyone became enthusiastic. When were they sailing? Where were they going first? How long would they stay? And where did they intend to go?

David, painfully aware of Olivia's high seriousness, took the questions over lightly. They were going first to Paris, *he* intended to show Paris to Olivia. What did she know of Paris? What did she really know of Europe? Always the same old round, the same hotels, no chance to cut away from Grandpa and her mama, the inevitable cures at Hamburg or Baden-Baden, taking the waters, taking the aftercure, and home again. It was his intention to show Olivia a Europe she had never seen.

Olivia declared that he was right. In spite of her many trips abroad, she was quite ignorant of Europe, always going out with a maid in attendance or with Grandpa and Mama. "I have authorized him," she explained, "to plan our entire trip just as he wants to. What fun it's going to be for me to be in David's hands, to see Europe through his eyes, as though we were both of us going for the first time."

Questions, advice from the others ensued: There were cities that must be seen, the names of restaurants, of famous dishes, hotels that nobody had heard of, masterpieces to be rediscovered, palaces by no means to be overlooked. Were they going to Vienna, would they visit Schönbrunn? They must not miss the Low Countries and the wonderful Dutch and Flemish painters. They must not miss Chartres, or any of the great cathedrals, they must motor through the châteaus country. Everybody had a preference for something. It seemed as though the continent of Europe, with all its beauties and delights, was being offered up for David to enjoy. Granny nodded her head and suggested that David must be sure to see the fountains at Versailles. And Uncle Alex added that as soon as they were back, Olivia must take him to see Niagara Falls. There was an attempt on the part of the others not to laugh.

"I have placed the trip in David's hands," repeated Olivia. "What a wonderful courier he will make."

CHAPTER

7

Iт was a long time before Mrs. Drew returned, and old Miss
Willoughby, plunged in the tender recollection of Laura's
story, was suddenly visited by memories—apocalyptic, unforgettable.

She was on Fifth Avenue amid enormous crowds. De-
lirium reigned. The crowds increased, from the West Side,
from the East Side, pouring into the avenue; crude improvised
processions—carts, wagons, motortrucks bearing effigies of
Kaiser Wilhelm, joined the delirious parade. On the sidewalks
men and women greeted each other, weeping, shouting. She
wept, she shouted, for never had there been before such a
spontaneous outburst of joy and thankfulness. Peace had been
declared! The Great World War was over. Now (it was
another war) she was sitting beside her radio filled with awe
and excitement and a gradual exultation, listening to a spectral
voice recounting that epic transport of Allied armies establish-
ing their hazardous beachheads along the coast of Normandy.
Unaccustomed forms lumbered and loomed before her eyes,
landing craft like arks ejecting uniformed young men with all
their gear and tackle on their backs, huge cranes depositing
ungainly objects on the alien shore. She seemed to see the
whole monstrous apparatus of the war now being waged in
the vast arenas of land and air and ocean; squadrons of air-
planes as beautiful in their formations as migrating birds,

roaring through the air on their terrible missions of death and desolation, elephantine tanks blasting their way through dubiously contested battles, and the deployment of the formidable navies in all the seven seas. How could it continue? How long would the energies and brains of mankind be wasted on the organization of these satanic wars? And even as she asked herself these questions, she was once more listening to an announcement, a voice broadcast from mid-Atlantic acquainting the world with the stupendous knowledge that man now held within his hands the ultimate, the unimaginable weapon, which had for the first time been put to use at Hiroshima. What fears, what apprehensions too terrible to even analyze or comprehend had become our portion? And grasping, in the midst of such universal terror and calamity, at her little meed of human love and sorrow and forgiveness, she thought again of David and of the time before the severance of the relationship between them.

After Laura's intimate confessions, a new closeness existed between them. They had watched with an almost uncanny perception David's adjustment to the new life which Olivia with so much confidence in her ability to make him happy had set up for him. It seemed to them both that he knew just how to improvise the various responses that could best assist her in plotting and planning for his future and his present happiness, and all this gaily, humorously, as though to entertain them with the little dramas of his newly regulated life.

She remembered vividly and in all its details Olivia's carefully plotted dinner party, experiencing it all through Laura's sensibilities. It was her part now to stand aside and watch. The communion she had shared with David and their long habit of receiving and exchanging impressions must be ignored. Watching Laura's face she seemed to know of what she thought—had David succumbed to Olivia's determination to boss and manage him, or was he attempting gaily to adjust himself to Olivia's lack of humor? What worried her most was that all life's awards appeared to be so easily obtainable. The trap in which he was caught was not that of having to work for any advancement or even great success in his profession but of seeing that these prizes were already within his grasp. It was Olivia's complacency in the belief that all this would insure his happiness that must have made her tremble for the future of them both. How long would he continue to play the role in which Olivia had cast him?

She was at Olivia's dinner party. Looking around at the familiar faces, she thought how little anyone had changed. She heard the familiar sentiments, everyone acting in character. For what did we strive? To give, to get, to establish an identity? As for Laura, what more could she give or get, had the hungers in her heart grown less intense?

Closing her eyes, she repeated:

"The desire of the moth for the star,
Of the night for the morrow,
The devotion of something afar
From the sphere of our sorrow?"

And she heard the marvelous phrase in the *Kreutzer* Sonata, like a bird, singing, ascending, pausing on the brink of some imperishable bliss.

No USE TO try to work. Old David could not get his thoughts about his mother and his marriage to Olivia out of his mind. It was those words that Blanche had so impulsively cried out to him when he had asked her if she had forgiven him that had so completely caught him up in the revival of his past.

That trip to Europe! There he was, seated in his steamer chair, exhilarated by the fresh sea breeze and listening with delight to the sound of water slapping against the ship, while he awaited Olivia's return to the chair beside him. She was in their stateroom superintending the bestowal of their luggage, so that upon his descent he would discover everything in perfect order.

Why did he have this sense of joyful escape? From what was he escaping? Olivia's supervision of his career? As the breeze freshened and the ship headed out into the larger waters of the lower bay, he knew that he wanted to escape from all the opportunities that had been offered him. Success in his career was certain, and all the prizes that it took most men a lifetime to achieve were his already. Was there anything for which he had had to struggle? All had been provided for him on the golden platter of Olivia's wealth. But today he felt that he was going to reach for something he could attain without her connivance or assistance. What it was, he didn't know.

The passengers were beginning to appear on deck dressed for the voyage. Steamer chairs were being set up, and some like their own, with names conspicuously attached, were already in place. It was amusing to watch one's fellow passengers, most of them a dreary lot, but doubtless there would emerge among the crowd a few with whom one would be happy to associate. Exciting, exhilarating it was, the day so blue and the breeze so fresh.

Two young women approached. "Oh dear," said one, stopping in front of him, "this is the place we should have chosen." She looked at the name on Olivia's empty seat, examined the name on his. "Mr. and Mrs. David Hare," she said, and taking no notice of him, remarked, "In the absence of the Heiress I'll sit down, and here's an empty chair for you, Alice."

Amused at the accuracy of her pun and thinking ruefully that in spite of her change of name Olivia's presence on the steamer was already known to them, he studied the two young women carefully. They disregarded him entirely. From where they hailed, or what their social backgrounds might be, he had no clue. Their voices were undoubtedly American, though without local inflections or enunciations. They were not English, they had no foreign accents. Something about them gave him a sense they might have hailed from anywhere, nowhere, as much at home in one place as another, unattached but perfectly at ease. The world they made their own. The elder was the more beautiful of the two, with faultless features and a face structured with almost classical perfection. She was taller and more impressive than her sister. The younger, whose beauty was not so faultless, had about her something completely irresistible. Her face appeared to be a document that declared so much intelligence and humor that just to watch it was to keep one in anticipation of what she might be on the point of saying next. She had a dimple that was difficult to locate, as though its habit was to appear in different parts of her enchanting countenance, which with its appearance and disappearance had the effect of changing her aspect and her mood.

They were in the midst of a discussion, which they continued after they were seated. "I was never so surprised in my life," said the younger. "Just as I was about to smile and shake her hand and say how nice it was to see her, she looked at me blankly and turned her back."

"I can't believe it, Helen. Are you sure it was Olivia Wildering?"

"As certain as I am that you are Alice Brooks."

"She must be here with the old man and her mother. 'Grandpa' will not fail to know us."

"Queer," said Helen thoughtfully, "I wouldn't have suspected her of being such a snob."

"After all we did for them that summer in Geneva."

Oh, then, thought David, they didn't know that Olivia was married, and the pun was not as pat as he had thought. Would he dare to introduce himself as Olivia's husband and make excuse for her as best he could? As he was deliberating the question, two gentlemen arrived upon the scene, both dressed in yachting caps and white trousers, one of them their father. Their nautical costumes somewhat accentuated their rather rakish appearance, and he did not know why he was shocked, and it even grieved him to discover, that these charming creatures were so closely related to such a frivolous and dissipated pair of boon companions.

Although usurping chairs that did not belong to them, the two girls lingered where they were, questioning their father and the other gentleman, whom they both affectionately called Bobby, as to what they had found out about their fellow passengers.

"Who, by the way, do you think Helen just ran into?" inquired Alice.

"Olivia Wildering," interrupted Helen with a subtle gesture and a quick change of expression that seemed to David an inimitable caricature. "She cut me dead."

Their father shrugged his shoulders and Bobby, throwing out his arms, exclaimed, "*Mon Dieu, mais pourquoi?*"

"I saw no Wildering on the passenger list," said Mr. Brooks, assisting his daughters to their feet.

"Come along," commanded Bobby, "we have our chairs amidship, on the other side."

David watched them go. What an oddly assorted lot, he thought, and what exceptionally attractive girls. And then trying to make up his mind whether to go down to the stateroom and assist Olivia or to wait for her arrival on the deck, listening to the sound of the ship cleaving the waters, the throb of the engines, and enjoying the salt smell of the ocean, he gave himself up to the delicious sense of complete severance from the land and total commitment to the sea. He heard Olivia's voice. Adrift from all responsibilities and human complications he made an endeavor to orient himself. Jumping to his feet he assisted her to sit down, while there floated through his mind, gulls, ships, waves, beautiful young women, and a pair of slightly disreputable gentlemen.

"Where have you been, David? I thought I'd never find you."

"I've been watching my fellow passengers," he answered, as he laid a steamer rug around her knees.

"Speaking of passengers, I'm in an awful quandary—such an unfortunate encounter."

"I know all about it," he said, reseating himself.

"What do you mean? How can you know anything about it?"

"Oh, yes I do, my dear. You deliberately turned your

back on one of the most enchanting creatures I've ever laid my eyes on. You cut her dead."

"David!" she exclaimed, surprised and on the defensive.

"What's more, it seems that you were once in debt to them. I wouldn't have believed it of you."

"But how, but where? Do you mean to say you've seen the whole crowd?"

"Yes, I've seen the lot of them. The girl you snubbed, whose name is Helen, was sitting where you sit now with her sister Alice in the seat beside her. They were discussing the matter, and I was about to introduce myself and make an excuse for your behavior, when their father and his friend turned up and bore them away."

"I was taken unawares and when that girl you think is so enchanting rushed up to me, I saw in a flash our trip across the ocean spoiled. I did not want to be associated with that shoddy crowd, and suddenly before I knew what I had done, I turned my back on her."

"And so you cut the ladies who had once been kind to you?"

"How do you know they were kind to me? And did they tell you all about it, David?"

"They paid me no attention whatever; I merely overheard their conversation."

"Oh dear, it's most unfortunate."

"What was it that they did for you?"

"That summer in Geneva, when mother was so ill, they got a doctor in the nick of time, who rushed her to the hospital for an appendix operation."

"In short, they saved her life."

"Oh dear, I wish this hadn't happened."

"So do I."

"What can I do about it?"

"You can apologize."

"But how?"

"Say you remembered suddenly something you had forgotten in the cabin and turned before you'd recognized that it was Helen who had spoken."

"She'll know that it was a lie. And anyway, it doesn't matter; they care nothing about women. You wait and see: they'll have every man on the ship pursuing them in a few days. I can't abide their type. You see them often wandering around Europe. Nobody knows who they are, or where they come from."

"Be that as it may, I want you to apologize."

The voyage was spoiled for both of them. Olivia did not apologize. The Brooks girls made no effort to reestablish past acquaintance. As their cabins were on the same deck and they went at the same sitting to the dining room, they were frequently brought face to face. It was extremely painful to David to observe how scrupulous both girls were in avoiding either smiles or glances of hostility. They simply accepted the fact that Mr. and Mrs. Hare did not wish to associate with them. And having to share the penalty of Olivia's discourtesy became almost intolerable to him.

The weather was beautiful and the crossing unusually pleasant. Olivia, who had crossed on the ship before, was treated with extreme deference and homage by the captain, stewards, and officers alike, which only served to accentuate their exclusiveness. He longed to break through all the solemnity and deference, to join easily in the good comradeship and gaiety that prevailed among the other passengers but found it somehow quite impossible.

The Brooks girls disembarked at Southampton, and as the tender bore them away, David and Olivia stood at the ship's rail along with the remaining passengers who were waving their farewells; neither of them waved but stood together silently watching the tender steaming toward the docks.

Finally David took out his handkerchief and said, as it fluttered in the wind, "Fare thee well, beautiful Alice and captivating Helen," and with reproach in his voice that cut Olivia to the quick,

> "Fare thee well, and if forever,
> Then forever, fare thee well."

AFTER THE DEPARTURE of Alice and Helen, David was left
with a curious emptiness and desolation. Although excluded
from their society, he had watched and waited for their appearance. In the lounge he had followed them whenever opportunity allowed, for the renewal of his pleasure and delight
in observing them, listening, attempting to learn as much
about them as was possible. Every morning on awakening,
the thought of their presence on the ship had filled him with
expectation and excitement. He had not wanted the voyage
to end because he knew it must terminate this secret attraction that had so powerfully obsessed him.

Now they had departed, it was over, the excitement, the
expectation; but there remained the fact that he was on his
way to Paris and that, amazingly deposited within his heart,
was a sense of something lovely—lost, and yet to be depended
upon to heighten his response to every aspect of beauty and
delight that Europe was about to offer him.

His first experience of Europe—Paris—came rushing back
to the old gentleman—beautiful, intense. It was spring, the
weather serene. The horse chestnut trees were in blossom, and
the city lay spread out like some fabulous architectural garden
under the blue skies and the dissolving clouds. Always,
wherever he found himself, he was acutely aware that the city
had wrought in him the condition of a young man desperately

in love with the most enchanting woman he had ever encountered, his heart and his imagination nourished by her charms. Expectantly scanning the crowds, he was not surprised how many times the graceful and slender figure of some young woman transformed itself into the lovely image of Helen Brooks, no sooner to be identified than lost again amid the gala throng. Paris had with its gaiety and brightness, its invitation to joy, become an evocation of this entrancing young woman with her loveliness and grace, her laughter and spirited conversation. And it seemed to him extraordinary how he had managed while accompanied always by Olivia, to keep all this ecstasy and expectation to himself.

Their days were hectically occupied with sightseeing. They visited the Louvre and the Luxembourg. They went to Versailles and Saint Cloud in hired taxis, and assisted by Baedeker and Olivia's constant suggestions, to Napoleon's tomb and the Bastille and the Conciergerie, and in moments of relaxation and frivolity, drove in the Bois and spent hours at the sidewalk cafes. They explored the Latin Quarter and Montmartre. They stopped at the bookstalls along the quays. She was making, it was plain, a brave attempt to let him initiate her, as she expressed it, to a city she had never really seen. And though she planned each day and gave him a sense of living within a schedule he would gladly have broken, she did her best to make him feel that it was through his knowledge and initiative that she was seeing Paris for the first time.

"Oh, David," she would monotonously repeat, "what a wonderful trip we are having together. I never enjoyed myself so much." And whenever they visited the museums, she put herself under his direction as though she had no ability on her own account to respond to anything she saw. He would exclaim impatiently that he could not tell her what she ought to like, that she must discover her preferences on her own. To which remark she would invariably reply, "But, dear, as you know so much more about painting and sculpture than I could ever learn, I intend to rely on you to be my guide." She grew more and more convinced that his response to beauty and to art had become just another one of her marital properties.

He was surprised at his ability to experience an independent joy in the great masterpieces and the subtle influences of the European scene while continuing to endure her conversation as one might listen to the ceaseless buzzing of a fly on a faultless summer afternoon. Paris—Europe—he had the oddest sense of familiarity with all he saw as though he were journeying through some well-remembered country of his soul. This he could not explain but took great pains to hoard up for future reference and contemplation.

Much to his relief they ran into their friends the Budinots, with whom they began to share their expeditions, and when they left Paris they hired a car in which they traveled together through the chateaux country; and, succumbing to the delights of such luxurious travel, he played without protest the somewhat ludicrous role in which he found Olivia had cast him. Although he was the only one among them who had never been in Europe before, he was to his own amazement traveling through the centuries as though the countryside through which they passed had been a book with which he was already well acquainted, and so, to Olivia's great delight, he was able to act as guide and historian. They traveled through the valley of the Loire, they visited Amboise, Blois, and Chenonceaux.

It had been their plan to return to Paris for a few days before visiting the Low Countries, but when they reached Tours, the Budinots did their best to persuade them to change their plans and to continue with them to the south of France and then to Italy. "Oh, no," Olivia exclaimed emphatically, "that would be quite impossible. David is determined to go first to the Low Countries, where before traveling further he wishes to become acquainted with the Dutch painters."

"That's entirely your own idea, Olivia," he had interrupted. "I never expressed any preference whatsoever. In fact, I think that Italy is a fine idea."

"Impossible," again declared Olivia.

"But why?" all three inquired together.

Astonished at finding it necessary to explain, Olivia went on to say that she had told David a hundred times that this was his trip, and she was carrying it out in every detail according to his wishes and desires.

"Meanwhile," said David, allowing the words to slip out before he could stop them, "consulting a timetable already indelibly made out in your determined little mind," and profoundly regretting his words, he had waited for Olivia's reply.

She continued as though she had not heard him, to explain why a trip to Italy was impossible. And to make his situation more distressing, he saw the Budinots exchange a wink. Nobody went to Italy in summer, it was too hot, she said, and thereupon ensued a long discussion about the advantages and disadvantages of traveling in Italy in summertime. It was no hotter, the Budinots averred, in Rome than in New York; the Romans, moreover, always enjoyed a long siesta in the middle of the day, and in the afternoons the galleries were cool and quite delightful, and the same thing could be said of Florence. Italy, Olivia firmly announced, was to be reserved for a second visit; David could not take in too much at one time. She did not turn to him for approval or disapproval but merely asserted her determination to carry out the trip according to the schedule she herself preferred.

That evening after dining, they said good-bye to the Budinots, who were leaving the next morning for Provence. When they were alone in their bedroom, David saw that the obviously dignified but injured reserve that Olivia had main-

tained was about to break down completely. "It was very un-
kind of you, David," she said, "to infer to the Budinots that
I was making all the arrangements of our trip in my own
'determined little mind.' You know quite well that everything
that we have done together has been in deference to your
desires."

He had hurt her, he knew, and he told himself that he
owed her an apology. "Yes, I know I shouldn't have said it,
Olivia, I apologize." Then suddenly urged by grievances too
long suppressed, he added, "But you make such a damn fool
of yourself." He could have bitten off his tongue.

"Don't you think I didn't see the wink the Budinots exchanged. I don't understand it, David, I don't understand
anything about it." She began to cry. "I have done my best to
make your first trip to Europe everything it ought to be and
to give myself in return the benefits of your enjoyment and
your education and your love of art"—she was sobbing bitterly
—"of everything I value in your character and background."

What had occurred? Where was this conversation lead-
ing? He seemed to see the structure of his married life falling,
crashing around them both. "Don't cry, Olivia. For God's
sake, don't take it all so tragically. Let's get things clear between us. Can't you see that the way you carry out your plans
and projects in the name of my desires and preferences, without being sure just what they are, often gets on my nerves?"

"Oh," she wailed, "you love the Dutch painters, you
wanted to visit the Low Countries." She sat on the edge of
the bed, the tears streaming down her cheeks. "David," she
cried, "you've spoiled my happiness. I thought our trip to
Europe had been so beautiful."

He sat down beside her. What could he say to this complacent, humorless woman who cared for him so much and
was in love with this image of him that she had so assiduously
built up? He took her hand.

"It's no use," she said, continuing to sob. "If I get on your nerves, I might as well go home and leave you to enjoy yourself alone."

Hopeless, hopeless, he thought, wondering what use it was to try to tear down her self-deception and complacency—what would she be without these attributes? If he tried to change her, he would destroy her.

She continued to weep.

"My dear," he said, "I'm sorry. The trouble with us is we don't quarrel often enough; we should quarrel oftener."

"What do you mean by that?" she asked.

"All married couples know that quarrels clear the atmosphere."

"Of what?" She would not let him off.

"Of pretending to be perfectly married couples. No marriages are perfect."

"Oh, David, I try so much to please you."

"I know you do, my dear, but don't you sometimes assume you know too much about what is likely to please me?" Oh God, he said to himself, here I am going through it all again.

"I don't know what you mean. I never said that marriages were perfect. And I do not like to quarrel," she said with emphasis. She got up from the bed, dried her eyes, and turning her back upon him, began to pack her suitcase for tomorrow's journey.

After some moments he rose and went to her. "Forgive me, Olivia. I do not want to hurt you," he pleaded.

"But," she persisted, "you didn't *really* want to go on with the Budinots to Italy."

"Not enough to make you cry about," he said, and seeing she had won the day, he made up his mind not to shatter the structure of a relationship he had so rashly attempted to correct.

CHAPTER

10

WHEN THEY RETURNED to Paris they kept the car a few days longer; they dismissed it before starting for Belgium and Holland. Whenever it was necessary to discuss their plans, Olivia made a show of leaving minor decisions in David's hands, but as the larger schemes had been already settled, he bowed to them with no further protest although her plans were roundabout and arbitrary.

They were sailing from Trieste in September, and a fortnight in Venice was to precede their departure. They had no further quarrels, but David was aware that his attempt to explain the imperfections of their relationship had dealt a blow she was unable to conceal. He gave himself up as much as possible to the enjoyments of travel. He had not been at all prepared for the impact of Europe upon his sensibilities. It invited him to leisure and the cultivation of his tastes. And it had begun to persuade him that the career he had chosen, the future already lined up, offered him no challenge and no congenial goal. Had he been free to choose his own career, what would it have been? Lacking, as he knew he did, the gifts of a creative artist—a painter, a poet, a musician—where could he find expression for all this wealth of unexplored potentialities that Europe had so mysteriously awakened in him? He was at a loss to know. Meanwhile let him enjoy the moments; one went in and out of them, accumulating memories on which one was dependent for insight and perception.

And what an awakening to himself this journey with Olivia had been! She was his constant companion. Although she had been in Europe many times before, she professed to find this trip full of new experience, and she depended upon him for enjoyment and stimulation. They ran across no further acquaintances, and it gave her a great deal of satisfaction to see how diligently he pursued the study of the great Dutch masters. "It was so much better," she kept insisting, "to have come here before going to Italy."

And to his questioning, "Why?" she always told him that Italy must be saved for a later trip. And when he protested that they were to have a fortnight in Venice, her reply was invariably the same: "Venice is different. It is a trip to Venice, not to Italy."

Indeed, here Olivia was right. Venice, so detached in its history and geography from the rest of Italy, a city like Aphrodite sprung from the sea, with its palaces and domes and campanile washed in the mists of pale lagoons and distant sea horizons, had, as it appeared to them in those early September days, an unreal, dreamlike quality, like some aerial theatre in which he and Olivia had their parts to play; for wherever they were, or whatever they might be doing, they had a sense of being set in motion, like all the other personages on the stage, by some invisible and skilled director with an eye to all their movements and the perfect congruities of the entire scene. Floating about in their gondola between the rows of ancient, crumbling palaces, every gesture seemed theatrical—the lighting of a cigarette, the movement of an arm, exclamations of delight; and even the sound of their voices mingling with the songs and street cries made them a part of larger spectacles and choruses. A gondola was always at their disposal. They went to Murano and Burano, and they spent a day at the Lido; they walked across the tiny bridges;

they visited churches, palaces, and museums. In the evenings they joined the other gondolas on the Grand Canal and listened to the nightly songs.

The days slipped swiftly by and with the recognition that the European expedition was all but over, David's spirit revolted against the thought of returning to America and the prospects awaiting him in New York. Olivia was beginning to talk about the plans for their return. The house would be, she declared, in order for them and the cool autumn days would be propitious for his return to work. She stressed heavily the idea of working hard, as though these months of pleasure should be followed by a strenuous pursual of his duties at the office. "You know, you have your name to make, my dear," she would frequently admonish. What kind of a name did he care to make for himself? To what had these months invited him, he wondered. This, the last of the European cities, had given him a sense of unsubstantiality, as though Venice itself, the Piazza San Marco, the Doge's Palace, the campanile and the cathedral, San Giorgio, and the Salute, the Grand Canal, with all its multicolored palaces, were about to dissolve, leaving him somewhat uncertain as to where he had been and what was going to happen next.

On the last afternoon of their stay in Venice, when the packing was accomplished, already arrayed in the costumes in which they were to travel to Trieste, David suggested, after a final visit to the cathedral, a cup of tea at one of the small tables set out near the Doge's Palace in the Piazza San Marco, where they could enjoy for the last time the shifting pattern of the crowds displayed so theatrically against the architectural splendors of that spacious promenade.

As they were hunting for a table they heard familiar voices. "Hello, hello there!" and turning, saw two of David's classmates seated at a table with two young women dressed in white. Both young men got up. "Well, think of meeting you here," they cried. "How jolly!" and one of them, who apparently spoke Italian fluently, ordered a waiter to bring another table next to theirs, urging them meanwhile to join them for tea, and before David quite realized whom they had encountered, he was aware that they had to meet a thoroughly embarrassing situation, for here were the beautiful Brooks girls and introductions were in progress. And as he and Olivia were presented to Helen and Alice, while wondering what reference was to be made to their presence on the steamer and how in the world Olivia was to meet the introduction, he heard the younger of the two, ignoring him completely, say, "We do not have to be introduced to Mrs. Hare because we met her some years ago in Geneva, when she was Miss Wildering. You remember, Alice, don't you?" And forcing on Olivia an embarrassed acknowledgment of the meeting, she amiably inquired if her mother and her grandfather were with them. "No," said Olivia, whom he observed was very disconcerted, "I am traveling with my husband"; and added that her grandfather and her mother were very well. Both Alice and Helen were glad to hear this, for Mrs. Wildering, they reminded her, had been so ill in Geneva. Conscious of the adroitness with which Helen had forced Olivia to acknowledge their meeting in Geneva and of her assumption that she had never laid her eyes on him, he heard her say, "But you must introduce us to your husband."

This, Olivia, although the introductions had already been effected, attempted to do. "David," she said, a little flustered, groping for her words, "these are friends I met in Switzerland. Let me present you to Miss Alice and Miss Helen Brooks." Bowing and observing a glance exchanged between the sisters, as though the two were acting in simultaneous accord, he declared that he was delighted to meet them.

The other table had been procured and seats provided. Tea was ordered, sandwiches and cakes. Everyone was seated;

and the young men, deploring the fact that they had not met before, asked how long they were planning to stay in Venice and could they not all dine together on the following evening. "No," Olivia made haste to say, "we sail tomorrow from Trieste."

Whereupon Helen, turning to him, while under the shadow of her broad-brimmed hat, the well-remembered dimple appearing and disappearing, asked on what boat they were sailing.

"The *Kaiser Wilhelm Der Grosse*," he replied.

"Oh, you like the German Line?" she asked.

"We always sail on the Cunarders," said her sister.

While Helen, giving him the benefit of a bewitching smile, inquired on which boat they had come and when they had sailed. These questions so quickly leveled at them made it apparent that the Brooks girls were taking the greatest delight in putting them on the spot. They exchanged a desperate look, while Olivia, seeing that there was nothing for it but to answer, said they'd crossed on a Cunarder early in May.

"Which one?" demanded the relentless Helen.

Forced to reply and cursing himself for telling the truth, David came out with it: "The *Mauretania*."

"Oh, how extraordinary! We must have been on the same boat," exclaimed both sisters together. "How strange we never met!"

So skillfully had they contrived to face them with their behavior on the steamer, albeit without reproof and showing no resentment but with extreme delight in their discomfiture, that it was impossible to know what next to say.

However, they were rescued from their dilemma by the young men, who had been so busy directing the waiters to set out the refreshments that they were unaware of their guests' embarrassment. Genial and ready to set the conversation going, they invited David and Olivia to give an account of themselves—where had they been and how had they spent the summer.

David, quite unprepared for the appearance of the lovely apparition, for whom all summer he had been consciously and unconsciously yearning and who, cool and distressingly triumphant, was seated at his side, found himself unable to reply. But Olivia, more prepared to meet the situation and attempting to regain her usual complacency, began addressing his classmates: "You know how much David knows about everything—architecture and history and art. Well, I simply put myself in his hands, and though he has never been in Europe before, my summer has been a liberal education." Trying to pull himself together, he heard his two friends, not without a touch of ridicule, praise the superiority of his mind. Unable to shut them up or to change the drift of the conversation, he was overtaken by a kind of paralysis. Olivia prattled on about their visit to Paris, their tour of the chateaus, their study of the great Dutch masters. And the girls, who were so much at home in Europe that conversing about the Dutch masters and the treasures of the Louvre interested them far less than the names of restaurants and the most desirable hotels in which to stay, managed to make Olivia's search for culture under David's guidance no more than a repetition of clichés already boringly familiar. What a cruel revenge they were having on him, ignoring his presence and at the same time making him conscious of being no more than a pawn in Olivia's hands. For had she not on the steamer induced him to ignore them utterly? How often they must have seen him silent and observant in the saloon while their gaiety and laughter entertained the group that always hovered round them. Had they known, or in particular had Helen, who plainly took the greatest pleasure in prolonging his discomfort, had an inkling of his secret infatuation and was she not definitely attempting, while she continued to ignore him, to captivate him further? How skillfully she managed, aided by her sister Alice, to keep him for so long from taking any part in the conversation.

Was he dreaming? Here was this bewitching girl for whom all summer long he had yearned, imagining he had glimpsed her among the crowds in foreign cities, now actually beside him, casting so powerful a spell upon him that he was rendered incapable of throwing it off, or setting himself free of its intolerable sweetness and discomfort.

"I am afraid our museum days are over—names, places," she said. "This picture or that, they merge with memories—a favorite Titian, a memorable Rembrandt, all a part of being here or there or somewhere else—of drinking a delicious cup of tea, the extravagant enjoyment of a view. You know what I mean, Mr. Hare. I expect I'm talking nonsense. Perhaps Alice and I have had too much of Europe."

The extraordinary thing was that he did know exactly what she meant. This young woman who sat beside him seemed to symbolize the intense delight with which Europe had taken hold of his imagination. She was Europe, Europe, and to have her reappear just as he was departing had enveloped the whole trip in his desire to see her again.

Who were these Brooks girls anyway, so much at ease with Europe, so much at ease with themselves and with the admiring young men who appeared at all times to be accompanying them? Had they no mother? Where was that dubious chaperon, their father, and his still more dubious companion, Bobby? Neither of *them* would be, by any standards Olivia held, regarded as gentlemen. Had anyone ever heard of them? If they were to turn up in New York, what place could they possibly take in society? These were, he knew, the questions with which Olivia fairly bristled as she continued her discourse on the great Dutch masters, and this was the attitude toward them, both girls knew well, she was maintaining. He was certainly leaving her in the lurch, and why was he so unable to come to her aid? "What?" he heard her say, "No, you've never been in Holland? We wouldn't have missed it for anything. David says that without a knowledge of the great Dutch masters, he would not have been able to understand . . . please, David," she said, "help me out. Just what was it you said about the great Dutch masters?"

He exchanged a glance with Helen, transitory, illuminating, for he knew that what she'd like to tell Olivia was that the great Dutch masters, for all he cared about them now, could go to the devil.

CHAPTER

11

No, said miss willoughby, she did not wish to go to bed so early, she would sit here and read awhile. There was nothing that she wanted.

"But," insisted Mrs. Drew, "you must try to prepare yourself for tomorrow. You need your beauty sleep, I'm sure."

"Yes," Miss Willoughby tried to conceal her annoyance, "I need all of that that I can get."

Bidding Mrs. Drew good night, she looked around the familiar room for she was back again in the old living room at Park Avenue, and it was not difficult to feel that she was exactly there for she had brought here to her apartment on West Fourth Street as much of the old furniture as the room could well contain. There in the corner near the window was Laura's grand piano, open as though she were about to sit down and play. The desk at which she used to pay her bills and write her letters was between the windows, and in the bookcases were many of the books that they had read together. It was a September afternoon, and she and Cousin Laura were awaiting the arrival of David and Olivia, who had just returned from Europe. And as she remembered her excitement, she told herself that one was never really old, for during the moments that one rehearsed the past, age dropped away and one could feel not only the reexperienced emotions but receive a vivid picture of oneself and one's surroundings. She was dressed in what she knew to be her most becoming gown and was aware that she was young and beautiful. There were roses in a bowl on the piano. The shades had not been drawn. One felt that summer lingered in the room.

Laura, dressed in gray, was expectant too but speaking in a voice that sounded troubled. She had not gone to the steamer to meet David and Olivia. Uncle Alex had been buried the day before their arrival in New York, and she had felt no inclination to gossip with the Wilderings, who she knew would have gone to welcome them.

"I wish he hadn't done it," she said emphatically. "I begged him not to. I'd known his intentions long before his death—poor Uncle Alex, poor, dear, perverse Uncle Alex."

Eagerly searching her cousin's face, she had asked her how she thought David would feel about it.

She was not so sure, she said. There might be something in Uncle Alex's belief that it always puts a man at a disadvantage to have his wife possess more money than he does himself, but David had a little money of his own, and would when she was dead, come into more.

It was easy enough to see that Uncle Alex's intention in giving David so large a part of his fortune was to disconcert Olivia. He didn't like her. He didn't like the match, and he loved David.

Laura rose and went to the window. "Uncle Alex's devotion to David has always been apparent," she said.

"And David loved him too."

"Indeed he did. When I used to criticize him and deplore his eccentric behavior, he used to say we couldn't have got on without him. He was the salt that lent savor to our lives."

"He was," Miss Willoughby remembered having said, "the most surprising and delightful figure in our childhood." And she heard Laura replying as she returned to her chair, that she was afraid that it was just another prank he had deliberately played against Olivia.

Perhaps. She could easily suspect him of it.

Laura heartily agreed but she wished he had not done it. It would in no way improve David's situation. He cared nothing about how Olivia spent her money and made no demands upon her for himself.

Suddenly old Miss Willoughby's heart was in her throat. The door bell rang, and conscious of her new blue gown and of her perturbation, she heard David's step upon the stairs.

He rushed into the room ahead of Olivia. He took his mother in his arms. She heard Laura, as she embraced him say, "I know how you will miss him, dear, impossible to think of life without him." And turning to her, she found herself included in his embrace. And for a few moments it seemed to all three of them that Olivia did not exist and had no share in greetings bound up in ancient memories and intimate affections. She stood excluded from their common griefs and memories but lost no time in interrupting their communion. Coming forward with an almost defiant cheerfulness, she said, "How fortunate it is that old Mr. Hare died so quickly and without pain."

Then Laura, kissing Olivia on both cheeks, replied that this was something they could all be thankful for.

She had been doing her best, Olivia said, to persuade David that this was no occasion for grief. "Imagine," she exclaimed, "the old gentleman paralyzed and speechless, pushed about by an attendant."

David, refusing to be comforted, replied that he would have liked to see him well and in his usual good spirits.

With considerably more than her usual tactlessness, Olivia demanded, "Why on earth did he leave David more than half his fortune when we already have so much?"

At this point all conversation was arrested, for Norah

entered the room and set her tray upon the tea table. She greeted David with enthusiasm, and much to Olivia's disapproval, he gave her a warm kiss. "Good afternoon, Norah," she said, and shook her hand.

As Laura poured hot water into the teapot, she said that it was wonderful to have them back and then when Norah had departed, turned to the travelers, suggesting there was much she longed to hear, adding that they both of them were looking splendidly.

And Miss Willoughby heard the young Blanche declaring, "We adored your letters, David. You seem to have fallen completely in love with Europe."

"My dear Mrs. Hare," Olivia persisted. "I know the motives that lay behind that legacy. David's uncle never liked me."

"And therefore," David asked, as though demanding an explanation, "he wanted to establish a rival dynasty?"

"It's not like that at all, David. How can you talk of dynasties? What's mine is yours and we already have too much."

Handing a cup to Olivia, Laura said that she should think that her little Laurel or David Hare II, was more than well provided for. "But whoever heard," she added, "of so much distress at having a fortune thrust upon one's family?"

"Oh," David interposed, "there are ways and means for me to remedy this misfortune, mother. Think of my poor relatives. There's Agatha and Cousin Lucy and what's the name of all those expectant European cousins? And Blanche," he added, laying his hand upon her shoulder, "How much of all this wealth will you consent to take?"

And here, to Laura's exquisite amusement, Olivia restrained her husband. "David," she admonished, "don't be rash. We must consult about all this together."

In the glance that she exchanged with Laura lay full

understanding of David's marital dilemmas, and that in trying to disguise from him their complete awareness of his situation, they must assume the responsibility of protecting this humorless girl from the ridicule to which she so habitually exposed herself.

Suddenly, although she had not realized David had seen the glance she had exchanged with Laura, she felt herself rebuked, as abruptly changing the subject, he launched upon an enthusiastic account of their European travels. He was back and it had begun again, this pretense that he did not know they knew all the secrets, the curious absurdities of his married life.

Sighing heavily and still conscious of her youth and beauty, old Miss Willoughby crossed the room, and switching off the light, thought with infinite gratitude that she would see him after all these years upon the morrow.

THE OLD GENTLEMAN looked at his watch. God! How long he had lingered over these memories! His first trip to Europe, with what vividness it had returned. That first sight of the beautiful Brooks girls, remembering every word they'd said, sitting there beside him on the deck chairs they'd appropriated. His response to Europe—so mysteriously merged with his remembrance of the two girls. And then that unexpected meeting with them in Venice; again remembering the conversation as clearly as though he had inscribed it word for word in memory. Well, it was late and he must get to bed. Tomorrow he'd see Blanche, who had forgiven him.

Dear Blanche, he thought, dear Blanche. How devotedly she'd loved his mother. And what a lovely creature she had been. He seemed to see her in that blue dress that she had worn the day that they'd returned from Europe. He sighed. And off he went upon another tide of memories.

How difficult his readjustment to New York had been. He had realized acutely that he had no gift for the profession he had chosen. Here he was, fettered to a perfectly fictitious legend about himself—a young man with a fine legal mind and a brilliant career ahead of him. He did not really care for the law, and he wished he had not made it his profession, better perhaps than banking, but he had no heart for it. The sycophancy and deference with which he was treated bored him to extinction. But more and more he found himself accepting the legend of his success and adopting patterns of behavior alien to his nature. How in the devil had he allowed himself to subscribe to assumptions against which his soul rebelled? It was Olivia's unawareness of his discontent that made him recognize how monotonous and repetitious all the situations of their life had grown. When he reflected on the breakfasts, the dinners, the cups of tea they drank together in the afternoons, the going to church on Sunday mornings, dining afterward with the Wilderings, the little dinner parties they gave, and the invitations they accepted, he realized that on all these occasions Olivia had somehow or other imposed upon him a catalog of conversational imperatives, and all of them conducive to a declaration of perfect matrimonial accord. How she prattled on about his abilities. He attempted to screen her absurdities by techniques of his own invention. Contrived as his behavior had been, lacking in all spontaneity, she delighted in it. There were the habitual clichés with which she explained him to the world. "David is so clever. How could one live without a sense of humor?"

And so behind this carefully constructed facade, life went on from month to month. Every morning she would declare at breakfast that in view of his long vacation, he must apply himself to his work with greater diligence. He was unacquainted with the personality he appeared to have acquired but continued to adapt himself to it as best he could, expecting that life would bring him neither pleasure nor surprise.

But then there had come that evening, when sitting together over their coffee in the drawing room, Olivia had suddenly restored to him the old spontaneous David Hare. "My dear," she had begun, "my dear," and there had been an expression on her face he had never seen before—a kind of shyness, a hesitancy and tenderness. And finally she had said, putting her hands before her face and bursting into tears, that there was something beautiful she wished to tell him.

He had guessed her secret. As though by some miracle his condition of apathy and boredom had been changed into one of sudden happiness—life had meaning for him, expectation. "Olivia," he cried, "how wonderful!" and rising had gone to her and taking her hands from her face had asked, fully aware of the profound wonder and mystery of the question, when she was going to make a father of him?

Quietly, almost humbly, she had demanded, "Are you happy, David?"

"Olivia, I am overjoyed! What news! What news! Olivia."

He had suggested that they go at once to tell his mother. She would be as happy as he was himself.

"No," she had declared emphatically. This must be their secret. They must keep it from everyone as long as possible. She had not and did not intend to tell her mother for a long time. She wept again, asserting that the secret must be theirs alone.

After this joyful revelation, his spirits rose; life had point and purpose to him now. The idea of fatherhood began to fill his mind. He had always been fond of children. Remembering his own childhood, the joy of being alive in a world so full of wonder and of interest in all that went on around him filled him with happiness. To think of sharing these delights with a child of his own brought him a constant sense of gratitude and expectation.

Conversation with Olivia became more interesting because of endless speculation about the new arrival and plans for the future of the child, whose sex not being determined, they could think of as either boy or girl and all the various arrangements made for either contingency. However, Olivia, always certain that her plans and projects would come out according to her own desires and directions, was perfectly sure that they were going to have a boy. "I am positive of it, David," she insisted, having already named and christened him in her imagination "David Hare II."

She was bewilderingly full of plans about her confinement; and her determination not to go to a hospital set her at once to planning for doctors and nurses and the installment of all manner of surgical appliances in her own home. Amazed at the details of her preparation for an event still many months away, he lent himself to her elaborate plans without protest. He was concerned about her health and insisted on her taking long walks every day.

It continued to be a disappointment to him that Olivia was unwilling to allow him to divulge what she called their "great secret" to his mother. And for a long time after her appearance had made her condition apparent, he was still commanded to keep his silence.

"POOR CHILD," whispered old Miss Willoughby, thinking as she got into bed, of little David and of the young man whose bones lay bleaching at the bottom of the South Pacific Ocean. Remembering that time so long ago when, as a young woman, she and the beloved cousin used to sit and talk of the precious baby whose advent had for so long been kept a secret from them both.

Laura had as a matter of fact divined his coming almost before Olivia was aware of this herself. And they had both known by the sudden change in David's mood and behavior that he was overjoyed at the news of the great event awaiting him. They discussed the subject exhaustively.

Why, she would demand of Laura, did he subscribe to all this silence? What had happened to his sense of humor— clinging so tightly to a secret which his behavior gave away on every occasion he came to visit them?

Well, Laura would say, she found him rather touching. Being so willing to concede to all Olivia's whims. It was her moment and he would not falter in his loyalty to her desires.

But she would insist that David should let his mother in on at least a share of all these preparations.

And Laura would reply that she expected, after the great event, to have an occasional look at her grandchild, but often wondered wistfully if poor David would be caught up in new rules and regulations.

They both agreed that Olivia was training him proficiently.

There had been that evening in the early spring when Olivia and David had been dining at Park Avenue and the conversation after dinner had been suddenly interrupted by Olivia.

"My dear Mrs. Hare," she had exclaimed, "how in the world have you learned that I am going to have a baby? And who," she asked, glancing at David as though he had betrayed her, "has let you into our great secret?"

Laura, unable to control her laughter, asked, holding up a tiny jacket she was knitting, how could she have failed with such conspicuous evidence at hand, to learn it for herself? Adding, that as her eyes had not been able to inform her of the sex of her first grandchild, she had hazarded the guess that it would be a boy. Blue was, she believed, the color bestowed on little boys.

Olivia, looking at David, inquired with astonishment, "Is my condition so obvious already? You should have told me, David."

He laughed, and as though to excuse himself from any blame in the situation, told her that he was waiting for her to realize this herself. And feeling that this public acknowledgment of the open secret had been more like a blunder in diplomacy than a natural occasion for family congratulations, remarked that all that was left to be revealed was now the sex of his unborn child.

"David, you know," rebuked Olivia severely, "that I am already certain I shall bear you a son."

"Good for you, Olivia! Stick to your guns," said Laura, and going to her embraced her warmly. "As I make it out," she said, "your young David will be born in May. That is the month my little David came into the world."

Wishing to declare the inaccuracy of Laura's calculations, Olivia announced that she was hoping for an Easter child.

"Our baby will be born," said David, "exactly at nine forty-five P.M. on Easter Sunday."

And as though he had established her infallibility, Olivia said that she was doing her best to prove that he was right.

After they had both departed, she had demanded, unable to control her laughter any longer, "That Olivia! How did the Wilderings ever dream her up?"

"Don't ask me," said Laura. "Jane Austen is the only person I can think of capable of such a masterpiece."

The period of waiting for the arrival of Olivia's child was extended until long after Easter had come and gone. And then one morning in May, they were both surprised, while they were breakfasting, to see David appear in the dining room, worn and haggard. Olivia, he told them, had been in great distress all night and was in the midst of what the doctor had told him was going to be a terrible ordeal.

"She was behaving," he said, "magnificently."

Blanche saw Laura rise from the table, and kissing David on both cheeks, say to him with great conviction, "She is brave, my darling, and because of her great courage everything will come out victoriously."

Remembering the little girl who had stood up with such amazing courage to Mr. Pierson's bull, old Miss Willoughby closed her eyes in an attempt to keep back the tears.

THAT WAS, thought the old gentleman, an unforgettable experience.

He remembered taking his son from the arms of the nurse. The child was screaming and his small, wrinkled countenance was so distorted by his screams that his red, enormous, open mouth was the only feature it was possible to distinguish. He regarded him with a variety of emotions. Pity, as he made it out, was stronger than love, but the sense of proprietorship mastered him completely. Here, though very much beat up, he was, and according to reports a miracle of obstetrical efficiency. If he had not now held him in his arms, what a loss, what a disappointment, how purposeless his life would be!

"A splendid boy!" exclaimed the nurse.

"A good little soldier," he replied, thanking God for his survival and handing him back, not without relief at giving over into more competent hands the diminutive survivor of the battle he had just won.

What had he felt? His responsibilities were great. What were, he had wondered, the hereditary ingredients likely to form the character of his infant son? Or would this be more determined by his training and environment? Filled with a mingled sense of humility and pride, he rejoiced in his paternity.

Smiling grimly, the old gentleman reflected on the scant

opportunities he had been given to exercise his paternal obligations. To be sure, he as well as his mother were allowed to
discuss at great length which side of the family the child was
likely to resemble. His mother thought he had Olivia's eyes
and brow but whether the nose or chin resembled the Wildering or Hare side of the family, she was unable to decide.
Olivia however proclaimed a firm belief that he was and
would be every inch a Hare. "He was," she announced with
pride, "an exact image of his father." But having awarded him
this distinction, he was strictly debarred from every pleasure
he might have taken in the care and observation of his infant
son. Every hour was carefully scheduled and so many prohibi-
tions placed upon his being taken up or watched or fondled
that all his protests were in vain. She was full of faddish
notions. He was left alone for hours at a time. And when he
wailed and cried, she used to say it was good for his lungs.

He appeared to be a fretful and delicate child, and there
ensued a long period of anxiety. His loss of weight and constant crying were ascribed to far more complicated ails than
those of teething. Doctors were constantly in attendance. His
digestion was unsatisfactory. He had weak lungs. He must not
live so long at sea level; he should be taken to the mountains
for the greater part of every year. The decision was made to
build a small house in New Hampshire next to Miss Rebecca
Barnacle's establishment, which would furnish plenty of simple food and good rich milk for his nourishment. And there
he must live for more than half of every year at a higher
altitude.

Superintended by an excellent nurse and deprived of his
mother's constant supervision, he began at once to improve,
and whenever he returned to visit his parents in New York, he
seemed to be a vigorous and comely boy, asserting his right to
good health and excellent spirits. Pleased by his improvement
but greatly disturbed by the vigorous response he appeared to

make to life, she insisted that the companionship of his far too entertaining father combined with the doting attentions of his grandmother greatly overstrained his nerves. He was overstimulated, overexcited. It would not do.

"David," she would say, "you must remember what a delicate and sensitive child he is." And she would bitterly complain that she had to bear all the hardship of preserving his health and guarding him from overstimulation while he, thinking only of his own enjoyment, recklessly exhausted all his energies in play. Presently a tug-of-war was going on between them. Which methods should prevail? Was she jealous and aware of her own inability to captivate her child? And did she see with great concern his mother's genius for entertaining children? Watching her improvise little games to strengthen the child's wits and enlarge his imagination, she would repeat on her departure, "It's all wrong, David. It's all wrong. Neither you or your mother will assist me in thinking first and always of little David's health." Did she really think her way of keeping him strong and well was to deprive him of his eager zest in life? He gave it up.

How long could he stand against her determination to be always right? Slowly his interest in his boy began to diminish. Olivia appeared to have won. The child lived more and more within the limits of the rules she imposed upon his bringing-up. Doggedly he turned his attention to work at the office. He tried to interest himself in civic responsibilities. He was utterly bored with life.

Suddenly the old man got up and began talking aloud, trying to assuage a sense of guilt and sorrow that had become a chronic state of mind. "Poor little chap," he said. "Poor little David. Did you blame the father who abandoned you? Were you healthy? Were you happy? What sort of a young man did you become?"

Finally old david got himself to bed, but he was far from ready to go to sleep, pondering the fateful consequences of the casual choice that he had made when Olivia had asked him that morning at breakfast whether he would rather dine at the Plaza or the Ritz.

"Very well," she'd said, "the Plaza." She would engage a table, and he must be sure to be there promptly at 7:30. It was her habit to give her staff an evening off on Saint Patrick's Day, and she regarded their dining out together as a kind of annual festival.

He had managed to be there on time, and she was already waiting for him, quite unconscious of the fact that the bomb which was to break her heart but not the mold of her unshatterable character had already been placed beneath the chair on which she sat.

God, the old man thought, how life pranked and played with human destinies!

"Bravo, David, you're on the dot. How nice you look!"

She was in a gala mood, for she loved this annual outing and used to refer to it as "our little Irish festival." She was full of little sallies and humorous suggestions, not at all becoming to her and highly embarrassing to him. He much preferred her I-am-a-very-great-lady mood. They began immediately to study the menu, the headwaiter hovering between them, pencil in hand.

"How about some Irish stew or perhaps a platter of good old Irish spuds, garnished with shamrock?" suggested Olivia. "And of course," she added in the same facetious manner, "a quart of Irish whiskey."

The waiter, very serious and concerned in assisting them but managing an indulgent smile, asked if he could make a few suggestions. Would they consider turtle soup to start with?

"Perfect."

"Then filet mignon with mushrooms?"

"Couldn't be better."

"And asparagus with hollandaise?"

"Wonderful."

"Then perhaps strawberries and cream?"

"Strawberries, of course. And we must crack a bottle of champagne in honor of Saint Patrick," declared Olivia.

"Oh, Mother! Not champagne with filet mignon," he corrected. "We must have red wine."

The sommelier presented them with the wine list. "Chateau Lafitte." He pointed with his pencil. "A great wine! We have a few bottles in the cellar, 1910, a splendid vintage year."

"Let expense be damned, David. This is the wine we'll order!"

But he was not interested. He was listening to a voice. Where had he heard that voice before? This was surely not the first time. And where and at what moment had he heard that lovely, suddenly remembered laughter? He craned his neck and turned and there at the table just behind them, the beautiful, the captivating Helen Brooks. Without an instant's hesitation, and omitting to explain himself to Olivia, he rose and pushed his chair back and joyfully approached the redis-covered, the incomparable Helen. He took her hand. She smiled.

"We meet again," she said. "And how courageous you've become."

He was challenged, exhilarated. "Olivia is here," he said, "and sends me with her greetings."

"My foot, she does." And then the smile, the bright dimple, the lovely laughter.

He rushed the questions. Where was her sister? Where was she stopping? How long did she intend to stay?

She and her father were here, she said, in this hotel. Alice lived in Boston. She had married Bobby Gunn, whom she knew he would remember, and then detecting his surprise, his disapproval, demanded with her most beguiling smile why he had always had so poor an estimate of Mr. Gunn.

"Not at all," he assured her, "not at all." His French was, as he remembered, so fluent, and with a faultless accent.

That was, she said, what everyone remarked when he was mentioned. But then she added, "Come, I must introduce you to my friend across the table. Jack," she explained to the young man, "this is an old shipboard acquaintance with whom I crossed the ocean years ago."

An acquaintance? He had never known Miss Brooks to make acquaintances. She had her friends and her admirers.

"But it wasn't altogether his fault, or was it, Mr. Hare?" she asked, the dimple in full play. She met his eyes and smiled.

He held her gaze and laughed. "I can assure you it was not." They smiled. They were enchanted with each other.

"But I must not keep you any longer. Your wife, I know, is waiting for you." She put out her hand. "Au revoir, my friend," she said.

"Over the river, lovely Helen." He turned, hardly aware that he had left her. Had she too been implicated in this electrifying exchange?

He found Olivia waiting for him. She was very angry. There was an expression on her face he had never seen before.

"Why did you think you had to speak to that objectionable girl?"

"I do not find her objectionable. She is the most beautiful woman I have ever encountered."

"She is exceedingly ill-bred, and I think, David, if you are honest with yourself, you will admit she is not a lady."

"What do you call a lady? Someone who is capable of not recognizing, of deliberately cutting a person who once when she was in trouble offered her kindness and great assistance—is this your definition of a lady?"

She did not reply. She waited some time before she spoke again and when she finally spoke, her hands were shaking, but her voice was under control.

"I told the waiter to take your soup into the kitchen to keep it hot. He will bring it back if you care to have it."

"Forget it."

The silence was glacial, and then the waiter, without disarranging it, appeared, performing the rituals of his office with incomparable correctness. He lifted the cover from the platter which he extended for Olivia's inspection and approval. His obsequious posture, his facial amenities indicating that without a nod or a word of approval from her, it would be impossible to continue with the ceremony of serving her the filet mignon.

"Very nice," she said, without the flicker of an eyelash.

Congealed in the silence that had arrested him, he stood, still holding out the platter for Olivia's inspection.

And there, the old gentleman remembered, he might have remained forever for, of any part he took in the progression of that silent repast, he was completely oblivious.

The filet mignon was apportioned and disposed on either plate. It was removed. The asparagus appeared and was removed. The strawberries were placed before them and commended for their size and color. The coffee was consumed and finally the bill was officially presented.

He took it and, verifying the astonishing total, paid it, and rewarding the waiter with an extravagant tip, left the table and, followed by Olivia, left the dining room.

The little Irish festival was over.

16

THE OLD GENTLEMAN groaned, or was it ironic laughter that now escaped him? For he was remembering the two occasions when that treacherous poet within him had so cruelly betrayed him.

There he had stood in his black velvet suit beside his mother in that great palace of the Wilderings, with its marble halls and stairways, the marble figure and the fountain, the sound of splashing water, voices, children's laughter, and that miraculous music as though invisible fingers played silver tunes upon the air. Under what magic dome of pleasure was he waiting? What landscapes beckoned and invited? What illimitable enchantments—ancient forests, vistas, fabulous gardens, incense-bearing trees? And out of what dreams, what insatiable hungers, had come this highborn princess to whom he now was offering a little silver box? And by what grace of regal approbation had the little girl in white invited him to dance?

Hearing that laugh, seeing that face, had he not been again betrayed by all the beauty, the poetry, he had so long suppressed? Repeating her name, attempting to visualize her face, what memories of the Europe he had visited for the first time with Olivia had been evoked—ancient towns and fabled cities with their palaces and monuments and gardens, which were upon investigation buried recollections of her voice, her face, her lovely laughter.

To remember his madness was in a measure now to re-cover it again. Helen Brooks—his need to see her, to talk with her, had devoured him. He had been quite ready to shatter his domestic life, to forfeit all responsibility for his child, to deal his mother the severest sorrow of her life, to ruin his position in society, to throw all chances for a reputable career to the winds on the dubious chance of winning her love.

His life from day to day had been contrived, fictitious, bearing no relationship to the usual adaptations and routines. Olivia's coolness toward him had slowly thawed. She had not wished to refer to the encounter at the Plaza. He, however, with a refinement of cruelty had not allowed the subject to drop, continuing to urge her, out of civility if for nothing else, to call on Helen at the Plaza and invite her to dine with them, for she was here without her sister and was a stranger in New York.

She had asked where Alice was, remarking that she was the one she liked the best, or she had meant to say, the one she disliked the least.

Why, it had given him a brutal pleasure to ask, should she dislike them so?

She objected to women of their sort, she had declared. They had no women friends. They were out obviously to capture men. If she remembered rightly, they used to operate together. Helen must be at a loss without her sister.

Taking pleasure in his ruthlessness he had answered, "She operates alone," adding that Alice had married Bobby Gunn, whom he was sure she must remember.

Yes, she had remembered him—quite a disreputable creature.

"What was the matter with him?" He had spoken a fluent French. He had envied him his accent.

She was sure that he and his boon companion had ex-plored the pleasures of all the European capitals.

Now, he had told her, Mr. and Mrs. Bobby Gunn were settled down in Boston.

"Boston," she had repeated, "of all the places in the world!"

Thus their conversations went, which in lieu of having further access to Helen, had given him considerable satisfaction.

Each day he had left his office early and walked around the hallowed precincts of the Plaza, but he never so much as caught a glimpse of the beautiful apparition he had gone to meet. What could he do to change his situation? Might he go to Blanche to ask her to help him out, to call on her and thus through her to establish a connection?

A damned fool idea. He'd best forget it and go home. Then suddenly retracing his steps, he had turned and walked into the hotel, crossed the lobby to the desk and inquired if Miss Brooks was at home.

The clerk opened the book, leafed the pages, and finally remarked that Miss Brooks had departed that morning for Boston.

Appalled, he inquired, did they know if she would be returning, and if so, when?

The clerk could not tell him.

Had Mr. Brooks, her father, gone with her?

"Yes," said the clerk, "they had gone together."

Spring, thought the old man, overwhelmed by the accumulated memories of springtime in his childhood, boyhood, and adolescence, the poignancy of its approach, that foreknowledge of the heart's capacity to experience joy and pain. "She was the spring," he said aloud, remembering that April afternoon when walking up Fifth Avenue he had, after weeks of waiting, so unexpectedly encountered her. Her dress, her flowered hat, the loveliness that like an aureole enveloped her, was only to be compared with spring itself.

Her greeting was spontaneous and touched with unexpected warmth. "How delightful!" she had said, and meeting his embarrassed but overjoyed response with easy grace, had seemed herself to have maneuvered his hailing a taxi, assisting her in, seating himself beside her, and ordering the driver to take them to the Plaza.

CHAPTER

17

Rᴇʜᴇᴀʀsɪɴɢ ᴛʜᴇ ᴅᴀʏs that followed, it was her face he saw again as it had then appeared to him, expressive and secretive at once, as though aware of the self-exposure involved in the human encounter itself. What with her dimple and her laughter and the charming interruption of an occasional stutter, one received the sense of her swift response to all the personalities to whom she was exposed.

He had as often as he dared called at the hotel to see her but had never found her alone. Her old friend Jack was usually there and various other young men he had never met before. She and her father had a sitting room that faced the park, quite impersonal and with every sign that its inhabitants were on the wing. Tea was usually served, and he always left restless and dissatisfied with his visit. She distributed her attentions quite impartially, and he was never without a disturbing realization that she was ready to share with any of them the little nuances of social intercourse that seemed in some peculiar way to put them all at some slight disadvantage. Was she flirting, or was this the sense she always gave him, that she found in each one of them an inexhaustible subject for gaiety and laughter?

It was very frustrating indeed and he found himself yearning for more private and personal encounters. With what vividness he remembered that lovely afternoon when he had run into her quite unexpectedly at the entrance to the park.

To his surprise she had met him joyously. "What an unexpected pleasure," she had exclaimed. She was longing for a congenial soul to share with her this perfect afternoon. Could he be persuaded to take her for a drive? The trees in the park were breaking into leaf and bud, and she continued her invitation by suggesting that they hail a taxi and get at once into the park, and if such a thing were possible, out into the country right away from all the rush and rattle of the city streets. The encounter and the invitation had been so unexpected and he had been so intent on hailing a cab, getting Helen seated, and giving directions to the driver that it was not until he found himself in the park and comfortably ensconced beside her that he was completely aware of his delight in this sudden answer to his prayer. Here he was, not only reveling in the budding trees, the soft spring air, but in this exquisite contact, this climate he had never breathed before, the fragrance of her light spring garments, every vibration, it seemed to him, of the warm, the living woman at his side.

She expressed great joy at the speed with which spring seemed to have overtaken the entire park. Pointing to a magnolia tree, she cried, "How lovely, with that ring of big white petals on the grass." Then suddenly, turning to regard the procession of passing cars, she exclaimed, "Why, look, isn't that your wife in that great limousine?"

Catching a swift glimpse of Mr. Wildering's car, the driver and the footman in plum-colored livery and Mrs. Wildering and Olivia with little David between them, he'd admitted that it was.

"And was that your little boy?" she'd asked.

"Yes," he had said. "It was."

"I didn't know you had a child," she ventured.

Had Olivia, he had wondered, seen them? For a moment

a temporary gloom had been cast upon his happiness. But she had let the subject pass, and he relapsed into full enjoyment of his situation. Why think or care about Olivia? He was here beside her in this car.

They drove through the park, up Riverside Drive, and presently found themselves amid wider horizons, assailed by a more intimate sense of spring. Her joy in natural beauty surprised and moved him deeply. She seemed to have a gift for the poetic phrase. The budding trees on the air with their delicate tints and colors reminded her of seaweeds spreading out beneath the waves. And all these sudden exclamations were thrown out amid running comments on her life.

He had, as he remembered, started to unwind her little story by asking if she did not greatly miss her sister Alice. The intensity of her response had astonished him. Why, he could not possibly imagine how she had missed her—every person, every human situation, every lovely view and room and railroad station they had excruciatingly (that was the word she'd used) experienced together.

They had had, though he had never seen her, another sister, Beatrice, who was now in China. She had married an Englishman who had business connections in Hong Kong. She was a beauty. But a perfect beauty. She and Alice in comparison to her were a pair of ugly ducklings. However, they were always called "the beautiful Brooks girls," knocking about all over Europe, first at one hotel and then another. "The Misses Nobody," from "Nowhere," the kind of Americans nobody cared to notice. Of course there were, she'd added, plenty of young men only too happy to accept them. They'd laughed a great deal and been very gay and merry, pretending not to notice their exclusion from polite society, the frosty nods and the cold shoulders.

He had winced at the swipe she'd taken at Olivia's behavior on the steamer, but had said nothing of this, asking instead if they'd always been chaperoned by their father; where was their mother; was she divorced from him; had she died when they were young?

Their mother, she had explained, had been at Davos at the time of her death. Alice and she were at boarding school in Switzerland. Beatrice was in Davos with their mother. After the burial, she had accompanied their father to Vevey, where they had taken her and Alice out of boarding school. After that, and how well he remembered her expression when she'd said it, the three beautiful Brooks girls had begun their notorious career all over Europe and, she had added, on the Atlantic Ocean.

And now, he'd said, restraining his emotion with the greatest difficulty, that she was the only one of the beautiful trio left, what did she intend to do?

She supposed, she had answered reflectively, that she ought to get married. There were a number of young men who'd invited her to do so, but she wasn't sure that she wished to avail herself of any one of these generous invitations. The thing she wanted most to do was to go to China to visit Beatrice, but she was afraid that was out of the question—her father disliked his son-in-law and he hated Hong Kong and he wasn't likely to pay her expenses if she started out alone. She found it difficult to know just *what* to do.

It was with the greatest difficulty that he had restrained himself from taking her in his arms and telling her that he adored her. That there was nothing in the world that would give him greater joy than to take her to China or to Timbuktu or anywhere on earth that she desired to go. But instead he only said, much to his own surprise, "China! Don't go so far away."

He needn't worry, she had assured him. There was little chance of her ever getting there. And changing the subject abruptly, she began to ask him questions about his little boy.

Then, at her caprice, he allowed the conversation to move from subject to subject. And presently they were on their way back and he was conscious only of her closeness to him, her fragrance, her laughter, and the inflections of her voice, and of his great desire to take her hand in his and hold on to it until the drive was over. Concocting all the while fantastic plots and plans and listening to a voice that whispered to him, "China, China."

After he had deposited her at the Plaza and dismissed the taxi, he walked the short distance to his house. As he let himself in his front door he wondered vaguely if Olivia had seen him driving in the park with Helen. It didn't really matter much. He found her in the drawing room already dressed for dinner. She reprimanded him severely as he poked his head in the door to tell her that he would be down immediately.

"You are late," she said. "I was expecting you for tea."

He didn't know it was so late, he would be down, if she would excuse him, in just a moment. He hurried upstairs. He had no time to change into a dinner jacket but washed his hands and face and brushed his hair, and on his arrival in the dining room, found Olivia already seated at the table.

She was, he noticed, more elaborately dressed than usual. (Had they, he wondered, an engagement for the evening?) She appeared to be very put out with him. She asked him why he hadn't telephoned.

Irritated, he said that he had been very busy at the office, she couldn't expect him to be always rushing to the telephone. Had she or had she not seen him with Helen in the park? Well, he thought, if she had caught him lying to her, let her lead him on the further prevarications.

"I want you," she continued, speaking very distinctly, "to make it a rule to telephone me at what time you expect to be at home."

"Heavens, Olivia," he had replied, he couldn't conform to any rule like that.

"Do you intend to completely neglect little David? The only time you have to see him is in the afternoon before he goes to bed."

He made no reply but addressed himself to his dinner and allowed the silence to continue just as long as she wished. She seemed to have made the same resolution—the soup was finished and the duck was taken from the table before she broke the intolerable silence and began to converse about indifferent subjects in an apparently amiable voice.

Surprised at her change of mood, he did not himself feel inclined for either talk or amiability and allowed her to bear the brunt of the conversation. When they got up to leave the table, he was astonished when she took his arm almost as though she mutely implored him not to cause her so much humiliation and distress.

When they had their coffee in the drawing room, he made no effort to fall in with her propitiatory and appealing mood but got up suddenly and went to the piano and began absentmindedly to strum upon the keys, while she, taking up the embroidery she had been working on before dinner, lapsed again into silence. Finally, aware of his cruelty, he rose abruptly, saying he must excuse himself for he had work to do. She need not wait for him.

He went directly to the library, and throwing himself down upon the couch, lay there motionless for hours, attempting to relive that drive with Helen in the taxi and to reassemble word by word all that she had told him of herself. Finally he got up and began pacing the room. Then going to the window, he pulled up the shade. It was late. All the lights were out in the neighboring houses. No one was on the streets. It rained.

He couldn't stand here all night, he thought. So turning

out the light, he stumbled to the door and groped his way upstairs. He found Olivia asleep. Without bothering to undress, he threw himself upon his bed and slept until the morning light was in the room.

CHAPTER

18

Mercifully, mrs. drew, who slept in an adjoining room, had ceased snoring and the sounds of traffic on Sixth Avenue had diminished. It was late and old Blanche allowed her tears to flow because they consoled her, deepening her great love for Laura in the remembrance of that May evening when they had been so close.

The weather had been unseasonably warm, and when on that late afternoon Laura had come in looking so extremely fatigued, she had guessed at once that something particular was on her mind. They had ordered tea just as Norah arrived to say that Mrs. Hare had called and should she come upstairs.

Laura opened her eyes and rising hastily from the sofa had said, "Of course, tell her to come up," and glancing at Blanche as though to say, why is she calling now, remained on her feet to greet Olivia.

As Olivia entered, she had seen to her utter consternation that Laura had fallen in a dead faint on the floor.

She and Olivia had run to her at once, and just as she took her wrist to feel her pulse, she had opened her eyes and asking for a glass of water declared that it was nothing, nothing at all. She believed that it was the heat that had exhausted her.

They had assisted her to a chair and she had continued to protest. She was, she said, entirely recovered. She begged

Olivia to remain for tea. Olivia excused herself. She had just dropped in, she said, to see if David was with them.

When she was gone, she had done her best to persuade Laura to let her call the doctor, but she had said she would not hear of such a thing—all she needed was a cup of tea.

As they sat there together, Laura had asked her if she could guess why Olivia had called at such an unaccustomed hour. She had not replied.

She had come, Laura said, because she was unhappy. And after a silence added, "Poor Olivia, poor Olivia."

"Poor David," she had corrected her.

In the silence that had followed, it had seemed to her that each was saying to the other, What will they do about it? What will happen next?

Finally, Laura, turning to her directly, had asked if she had any idea who the young woman could be.

She had hesitated and then had said the girl's name was Brooks, Helen Brooks.

David had never really been in love, Laura had said as though speaking to herself, and laying down her teacup, returned to the sofa.

There was a long silence after which she had risen and gone to her. Covering her with a light shawl, she stood regarding her. How fatigued she looked! She had changed a great deal since those early days when she had known her first, in full possession of her beauty. She was paler, her features were more finely drawn, her face was almost transparent and the fine structure of her bones more noticeable. How beautiful she was! How self-sustained, how valiantly she had disciplined her heart's perpetual desire for greater love than it had received. Her face was like a testament on which her virtues were inscribed. She bent and kissing her tenderly, went back to her chair and to her reading.

How well old Miss Willoughby remembered the book she

had been reading. It was by H. G. Wells, full of warnings and forebodings which had darkened her mood and her personal anxieties. European war was imminent. We were living in an age that we had made and were unprepared to meet. And as her thoughts kept wandering in and out of all his startling information—new inventions, new experiments—she had attempted to adjust herself to the conception of a future alien to her past and to her memories. The life behind her was so safe and so parochial. And thinking of her childhood, she remembered that old park and Mr. Pierson's bull and thought how David would tell his grandchildren how their grandmother had stood up to challenge him the day he slipped his tether. Speculating as to the possibility of his ever having grandsons, she had asked herself, what of the future, what of David, what of Olivia, and what of little David? And as she asked herself these questions, she had become aware that Laura was looking at her. She rose and went to her.

"I'm glad you came, dear," she had said. "There is something I want to tell you."

Fear had struck at her like a sharp blade, cutting a clean, incisive wound, filling her heart with anguish. She had guessed at once just what it was that Laura was about to say to her, and she had cried, "I know, you needn't tell me. I know just what you are going to say."

"Which will," Laura had said, "make it easier for me, dear child." The sound of the traffic, the breathless smell of the hot city, filled the room. Laura had waited for her next response.

Finally, reproaching herself bitterly, "Why didn't you tell me before?" she had cried.

"To have alarmed you with my fears would have caused you unnecessary pain, but now that I am sure myself . . ."

"I could have helped you. You need not have gone through this alone."

"We will go through it together now, Blanche."

"I should have known," she had kept repeating.

"Your knowing, until now, would have been of no avail. We will face the truth together. I am sure you will be brave, my dearest."

"Only let me ask one question. There is nothing to be done for you?"

"No," she had replied, "nothing."

"And David, when will you tell him?" she had asked her.

"I shall not tell him. I shall wait," she had answered firmly, "until he discovers this himself."

"But, Cousin Laura, you should tell him."

"No." She was resolute. "You must stand behind me in this decision."

Life with its ceremonies appeared to be continuing. Norah came in and announced that dinner was already on the table.

Mrs. Hare, she had told her, was overtired. Could she bring their dinner to them on a tray?

She readily complied and said she was sorry Mrs. Hare was not so well.

And while they waited for their dinner, they appeared to be quite calmly talking of their plans and readjustments. She had pressed Laura to tell her more of what the doctor had advised. She would be able, she had asked her, to spend the summer at Dune's End?

Alas, she had replied, Dr. Lawson did not wish to have her go so far away from him.

A protest had escaped her. It would be cool there. She loved the place so much. There would be other doctors near them, surely?

She had answered that he felt that under his care she would suffer less.

Again the stab of fear—the intolerable anguish of despair.

"My dear, my dear, we will not let you suffer," she had cried.

Laura had closed her eyes. "Dune's End," she whispered, "the smell of the sea, the sound of the waves, the gulls crying, and waking every morning to the song of birds—that music of the beauty of the world."

They did not speak again until Norah entered bearing their dinner on a tray. She set a little table near the window and lingered, hoping they would ask her to remain. She told her they would ring when they were ready for their coffee.

Their speech, when they were left to themselves, seemed trivial. They touched on the oppressive weather and its effect on Laura's health. Laura would be better, she had insisted, when the hot spell was over. They spoke of little David, who would be going to the country soon and said that he was looking well.

But the sorrow that encompassed their evasive conversation became at last too much for Laura, and she asked abruptly if Olivia's visit had not struck her as being odd—she never called at teatime. What was the purpose of her coming?

She had waited before answering, for she had also suspected that Olivia had wished to talk with them about her marital situation. They both knew how hard it would have been for her with all her pride to have humbled herself in complaining to them of David's behavior.

The distress in Laura's eyes was more than she could bear. "Poor David," she had finally said, "poor David."

They had eaten very little, and when Norah arrived with coffee, she had looked at their plates askance. "Such a tasty dinner," she had complained, "that cook prepared for this hot night." Shaking her head, she took the plates away, leaving them to drink their coffee.

Laura returned to the sofa and again lay down, and she lingered by the window. The silence was extended. Norah returned to remove the cups and went out. Remaining where she was, she kept her silence but finally became aware that Laura was speaking to herself.

Going to her, she had taken her hand. Of what was she thinking? she had asked.

She'd fetched up, without comment, a few arresting words: " 'Would pawn each atom that I am, for immortality.' " Adding then, with great intensity, " 'Oh, God of Width, do not for us curtail infinity.' "

Sitting down beside her, she had asked abruptly, "Are you afraid of death, my dearest?"

No, she didn't think so. She didn't believe in hell or the dreadful retribution of her sins. But those lines of Emily Dickinson's, about infinity, might, if anything could, explain just what she felt about it. "Star behind star, galaxies, planetary systems, myriads of Milky Ways, on and on in an interminable forever—think about it, Blanche."

And did this bring her any comfort, she had asked her.

It filled her, she had answered, full of awe.

"But all this seems so inhuman, Cousin Laura darling. Have you no belief in a personal God?" she had ventured.

"I don't think so, dear, only in His existence and the creation of His universe. Of the whys and wherefores of the human condition, which seem to me the strangest, the most poignant of all the earthly mysteries, I can only speculate. And why I should relate the miseries and joys I have experienced here, to this mystical sense I carry with me of God and His entire cosmos, I cannot explain."

"But are you ready now to die, my dearest?" she had insisted.

The fact that she must leave this world just now, was a great grief to her, she answered. In the light of the crisis David appeared to be approaching, it would break her heart to have him leave his boy.

But, she had protested, she was forbidden to tell David of her condition.

She had again implored her not to speak of it.

Once more the silence was prolonged. The May twilight had merged with the night and darkness. It was late; the room was lighted only by the street lamps and the glare and flash of motors rushing by. Laura's eyes were closed. The beauty and sorrow in her face filled her heart with a love so profound that she knew this evening would remain with her always as the deepest experience in her entire life.

Was she asleep or had she only closed her eyes?

THE OLD GENTLEMAN, unable to sleep, got up and raised a window shade that he might have a glimpse of the unfamiliar city beyond him in the night.

Watching the moon emerging from a cloud in a jagged section of the sky above his head, he remembered how the insane desire to see and to be with Helen Brooks had spun a web of deceptions and contrivances around his life which had made his conduct seem to him both mortifying and surprising. His behavior to Olivia had been dishonest and frequently deliberately cruel as though he had been trying to bring about a crisis in their marital relations.

His fear of losing sight of Helen again had been what drove him to such excesses. He was constantly telephoning, and if he failed to make engagements with her, attempting to pry into all her movements and to make out where she was and what she was doing at almost every hour of each day. He had wanted to get from her if possible some statement of her plans. He was obsessed by the knowledge that what she wished above all other things to do was to visit her sister in Hong Kong. It was this knowledge that had driven him to the completely lunatic idea that he might capture her affections and persuade her to elope with him to China.

Urged from within by these mad plans and impulses, he had hardly known himself. How callous had been his disregard of the wounds he inflicted on Olivia, and what curious strategies she had employed in the subtle conflict that went on between them! She made no mention of Helen, and she had ceased to reprimand him for his failure to return home at the usual hours, accepting his excuses of heavy work at the office and frequently insisting that he was overworked and greatly needed a rest, suggesting that before he broke down completely he should go with her to the country where little David was installed, or better still, forget not only his work but his family and go to Europe where he could enjoy the pictures and the museums quite alone.

His determination to see Helen as much as possible had been often frustrated. As soon as he arrived at his office he would telephone the Plaza. Would she have luncheon with him, and if not luncheon, tea? Could they take another drive together? The engagements that she made with him were always complicated by the presence of other admirers. There was the young man with whom she was dining when Olivia had first observed her at the Plaza and several others whom he had not met before. It was only on the rarest occasions that he had seen her alone, and his desire to hear her plans and to get further glimpses into her past was seldom appeased. Remembering her confession that what she really ought to do was to accept one of the proposals all these suitors had so generously offered her, he saw himself in a most disadvantageous position. His rivals appeared to be unfettered by marital obligations. He had jealously watched her behavior with them. Was she an incorrigible flirt? He had come to the conclusion that it was not a matter of a conscious attempt to captivate her victims but merely a spontaneous exhibition of her physical attributes. The expressions that flitted across her face, the appearance and disappearance of her dimple, the inclination to smile or laugh or listen, nothing about her was calculated or contrived. She enjoyed and was accustomed to the admiration of men, but she never attempted to provoke it. All this made her, he had decided, peculiarly impervious to falling in love herself. And the idea that he could ever be the one to take her heart by storm and awaken in her a sudden response to his passion seemed to him preposterous. How could he possibly foster his ridiculous plans and continue to pursue such unobtainable goals? He was an ass, a fool, he would tell himelf a thousand times a day. The thing for him to do was to withdraw, come to his senses and carry on the life already designed for him.

But of what worth had been his resolutions? He was obsessed by Helen and his pursuit of her. The plans that were constantly at work within him possessed his mind and his behavior. What could he do to make her feel that he could be of some assistance to her? He knew he was not unattractive to women. But if to procure her preference for him was the first necessity in the fulfilling of his preposterous dreams, how was this to be accomplished? She certainly knew that he was in love with her, but she took it for granted that all of her admirers were in a similar condition. However, he was in far more danger than they of being dismissed by an open declaration of his love. On the few occasions when he found himself alone with her, he constantly attempted to make her talk about herself, and his anxiety about her immediate plans did not escape her.

There had been that afternoon when he had gone to visit her and had been appalled to notice various steamship schedules and European travel brochures strewn about.

Were they planning soon, he had asked her, to depart for Europe?

This was a seasonal occupation, she had explained, shrugging her shoulders and throwing out her hands. But with Alice now married and living in Boston, the European expeditions had but little charm for her.

Suddenly, explosively, he had cried out that she could not. He would not let her go.

How well he remembered the gesture. She had shrugged her shoulders once again and asked, as though appealing to him, what else was there that she could do?

On the point of revealing his wild plans, his absurd proposals, he heard the key turn in the lock and saw Mr. Brooks coming toward them.

He was shocked at his appearance, and the thought of Helen always accompanied by a father so conspicuously déclassé caused him a moment of acute distress. She introduced him as the young man who had crossed with them on the *Mauretania* some years ago.

Hastily taking off his hat and looking at him somewhat mistrustfully, he had remarked that he could hardly have been expected to keep track of all the young men attentive to his daughters.

But, Helen reminded him, this young man had been far from attentive to Alice and herself. Did her father, she asked, not recollect Mr. David Hare, who had married Miss Olivia Wildering, whom they had known before in Switzerland?

Cut to the quick by the familiar taunt, he was, however, acutely aware that the old memory was so charged with mutual challenge and attraction that the glances they now exchanged suddenly conveyed to each of them the tremulous vibrations of their nerves. Excited by these secret messages, he said to Mr. Brooks that he had been, as his daughter had just informed him, an exception to the rule, and retaining the spell of Helen's glance in order to lengthen these exquisite sensations as long as possible, he had waited on her to continue. Could it be true that he had won the first round of this difficult conquest? Had these surprising signals, flashed from eye to eye, indicated that she too had been pierced by the same mysterious shafts of mutual attraction? She would not, he knew, meet his glance again, but was she aware of how much had been revealed to him?

"Doubtless," said Mr. Brooks, "they are all persuading you to stay, my dear. But," and he scanned a list of sailings, "our return to Europe is more than overdue."

"My father and I have been discussing," said Helen, not returning his glance and attempting to act as though those astonishing messages had never been exchanged, "the relative merits of Carlsbad and Hombourg. He prefers the former but I stand out for Hombourg. If I concede to him, there'll be the usual aftercure in the Black Forest, and then the choice is mine. Think of it," she added, "the whole of Europe— where to choose!" and she placed the folders she had collected on the table.

It had been difficult for him to pull himself together and make a coherent reply, and to his astonishment he heard himself saying, not to Helen, but to Mr. Brooks, "I understand your daughter would like to go to China, where she tells me she has another married sister."

"China," said Mr. Brooks irritably. "Out of the question."

He received a message, certainly not from Helen's eyes but from the expression on her face and the sudden stillness and rigidity of her posture, which very plainly was a reprimand. Abashed and hardly knowing what he was about, he said that he should not have intruded on the making of their plans and asking both of them (idiotically, he knew) to forgive him, he bade them good-bye and left the room.

All that evening and the night that followed, his mind had been in a state of turmoil. Elated by the memory of that electrifying glance and aware for the first time that there existed between himself and Helen a mutual intimacy and attraction, he now fully realized the issues that confronted him. For the first time since this fatal infatuation had taken possession of him, he asked himself if it would not be possible

to throw off its spell, to leave New York and remain in ignorance of the outcome of the plans of Mr. Brooks and Helen.
Did he not owe something to his son? Did he not owe everything to his mother? He forced himself to face her anguish
at his ruined reputation, his severance from all standards of
honor and propriety.

"Louise Denis, Louise Denis"—he seemed to see a gentleman with a black beard standing above her on the dunes and
then her gesture of rejection, and the name became a challenge
and a resolution. He would break the fetters of his desire for
Helen. He would not be enslaved by this intolerable passion.

He would leave New York the following day. In the
morning as he was about to tell Olivia that he had decided
to leave at once for a short vacation in New Hampshire, appalled at his failure to obey the commands he had laid upon
his tongue, he heard himself urging her to go without him.
He would follow, he told her, in a few weeks when the rush
of work was over.

"Do as you please about it," she had said quite calmly;
and then irrelevantly, she asked if he had noticed how ill his
mother had been looking of late.

"No," he said, forgetful of everything but his failure to
carry out his resolution. "What is the matter with her?"

Olivia said she didn't know, and she related in some detail how Laura had fainted dead away when she had called
on her in the late afternoon.

Unable to take in more than one idea at a time, Olivia's
story hardly registered. He had not thrown off his fetters; he
had failed in his struggle for self-discipline; he was free to go
on with his madness.

He had walked to his office deploring his weakness and
the general disintegration of his character but nonetheless
elated at his freedom to continue his pursuit of Helen, made
less hopeless now by the remembrance of that brief moment

of certainty. Yes, he assured himself, he had felt certain that she was attracted to him, indeed that she had sent out a signal of distress as though somehow she now depended on him to assist her, to understand her plight and help her in escaping from it.

When he reached his office, he had lost no time in telephoning the Plaza. Was Miss Brooks at home?

"No," came the prompt rejoinder, she had left, she was no longer there.

"What?" he asked, overwhelmed with disappointment and despair.

"Yes," came back the voice, "she left last night for Boston."

"Did Mr. Brooks go with her?"

"No," said the voice. "Mr. Brooks is still in the hotel."

"How long does he intend to remain?"

"I do not know, sir," said the voice. "Shall I connect you with his room?"

And before he knew just what had happened, he heard an irritable voice, "Yes, yes, who is it?" Not knowing what to say and abashed at having to improvise a reply, he hung up the receiver.

T HE OLD GENTLEMAN sighed profoundly, surprised at the accuracy with which he was recapturing his memories. He thought of time and change and of the world that had in his day and generation sustained such unimaginable changes and calamities and of Blanche, whom he would visit on the morrow, who had said she had forgiven him.

What was the meaning of it, why had Helen gone to Boston? Had some accident, some sudden illness occurred to Alice? God, what business was all this of his? Suddenly he got up. He again went to the telephone. He asked the operator to connect him with his own house.

"Hello, hello, can I speak to Mrs. Hare?"

"Very well, sir."

Waiting for her voice, he had wondered what to tell her.

"Yes, David, what is it?"

And then he told her brusquely he was going to Boston on the twelve o'clock. There were some depositions in the Snyder-Gardiner case he had found that he must take at once. No, he had answered, he'd have no time to come home first. What? Luggage? No, that would be unnecessary. He would be gone only a day or two. "Yes, yes, good-bye." He was in an awful hurry.

Astonished at himself and at the plan that he was making, he muttered, "The Snyder-Gardiner case? What the hell!" (Those depositions he must take—there were no depositions.) Scarcely aware of what he was about, he had gone to the office of his superior and told him that there had been a death in his family, and it was necessary for him to go to Boston for a day or two.

Appalled at the ease with which he was able to manufacture falsehoods to meet whatever emotional necessity made them useful, he took his hat and gloves and left the building. Out on the street and face to face with his resolve, he wondered vaguely how to kill the time till twelve o'clock. He might go to see his mother, and elaborating further falsehoods, tell her he was leaving for Boston on business for a day or two. No, he'd better not. Aghast at the madness of his behavior, he went to his club, where he attempted to sit down and read the morning paper.

A few minutes before twelve o'clock he was seated in the parlor car on his way to Boston. The die was cast, and what would be the outcome of this impertinent intrusion into the affairs of Helen Brooks?

As he asked himself the question, he became aware that Mr. Brooks was seated in an opposite chair.

Good Lord, what was the meaning of this—would he pretend he hadn't seen him? He didn't want him to think he was following his daughter. On the other hand, he longed to know the cause of Helen's departure. For some minutes he acted as though he had not seen him but finally rose and greeted him.

Mr. Brooks nodded and gave him a suspicious look as though he had guessed the reason for his journey.

Business, he said, had called him suddenly to Boston. "And you," he added, "may I inquire about your daughters?"

He had answered briefly, his daughter Mrs. Gunn was

critically ill. Turning his chair toward the window, he buried himself in his newspaper.

He had seated himself again, and abashed by his proximity to Mr. Brooks, got up and went into the smoking car, where, unable to confront the consequences of his lunatic behavior, he sat miserable and irresolute until the train pulled into the South Station.

Wouldn't it be better, he asked himself as he got off the train, to return at once to New York? But driven by his need to see Helen and the idiotic hope that he might perhaps be of some help to her, he walked directly to the Hotel Touraine, where somewhat to his surprise he engaged a room for the night.

The bellboy unlocked the door, gave him his key, and on entering and looking about him, he was sure that he was in the very room. . . . The twin beds, the prints on the walls, the bureaus and the chairs brought back to him with overwhelming impact the memory of his bridal night.

He went to the window and looked out on Tremont Street—Olivia, his marital relations, Helen, his need, his passion for her—the phantasmagoric strangeness of his life. What was he doing here entangling himself with lies, unpremeditated plans?

He turned and against all the dictates of his reason, left the room, descended in the elevator, and went directly to the desk, where he asked the clerk to look up in the telephone book the address in Brookline of Mr. Robert Gunn.

After receiving the number of the street and directions how to get there, he hailed a cab and committing himself irrevocably to his folly, gave the driver the proper address.

Arriving at his destination he told the driver to wait, and mounting the steps of a spacious brick house and filled with consternation at his audacity, rang the bell.

Nobody appeared to be at home. He rang a second and finally a third time. Just as he was about to leave, the door was opened by a maid, who was unable to give him any satisfaction in the answering of his questions. No, Mrs. Gunn was not at home, she was at the hospital. No, Miss Brooks was not there, she was at the hospital. No, she could tell him nothing about Mr. Brooks. Was Mrs. Gunn seriously ill? Oh, yes, sir, very bad indeed. Sure, sir, she didn't know, a hospital in Boston.

Descending the steps, he said to himself he'd take a shot at it. Then ordering the driver to take him to the Massachusetts General Hospital, he got into the cab and feeling as though he were enveloped in the scenery of nightmare, allowed the driver to conduct him to his destination. His feeling of strangeness, unreality, grew so acute that in the scenes that followed he never lost the sense that he was walking through a dream.

Had he stopped at the desk, or had he never inquired for information about the condition of Mrs. Gunn? Or was he suddenly confronted by three phantom figures wandering, as it seemed to him, through phantom corridors? And had he heard the voice of Helen greeting him as though his presence there was natural, saying in brokenhearted accents, "Alice is dead; she died on the operating table." And were the other phantoms Mr. Brooks and Robert Gunn? Was he offering them assistance? Had they, all three, put themselves into his hands?

And were the next three days a dream or a reality? Had he found himself at the undertaker's choosing an appropriate coffin, purchasing a lot in Mount Auburn Cemetery, engaging a clergyman, ordering the digging of a grave, following the funeral cortege in a close cab with all the shades drawn down, accompanied by Helen, Mr. Gunn, and Mr. Brooks, and lastly, standing in the rain with Helen at his side while the coffin containing beautiful Alice was slowly lowered into the ground?

When he returned to New York he had not been accompanied by Helen and Mr. Brooks. They had remained behind to help Robert Gunn in winding up his affairs. He had been so moved by Helen's grief and so determined to offer whatever assistance was in his power to give her that he had not given Olivia or his mother a thought. Now, he was returning with no information about Helen's plans. The only life he appeared to have was involved in her. She had been pathetically grateful to him for all that he had done, but her eyes had conveyed no reassuring messages acknowledging a mutual attraction. They had told him only that her heart was broken and that he could expect no more from her than gratitude. When she returned to New York there would be a new Helen and a new situation with which to deal.

It was late when he arrived at home. Olivia had dined and was reading in the drawing room. She had looked up coldly and asked him why he had had to lie to her about those depositions. Before he had time to answer, she had observed with a voice of withering accusation that she had seen an obituary notice of the death in Boston of Mrs. Robert Gunn. Had she seen a Boston paper? How had this information come to her? "Beloved daughter of Mr. Augustus Brooks. New York and Paris papers repeat," her voice continued.

What was there he could answer? "Yes," he had said, as though appealing to her sympathy, "that beautiful young woman is dead."

He had longed to break down completely and tell her of his desperate love for Helen and beg her for sympathy and assistance. But her accusation of his falsehood had suddenly turned into a mute appeal to him as though she implored him to tell her anything, anything but the truth, and was attempting to persuade him that his infatuation was a brief illness from which he would soon recover. They looked for a long time into each other's eyes, and presently as though she were ready to forgive and to forget, she changed the subject and asked him if he remembered what she had told him about his mother.

"What was it that you said?" he asked. And recollecting she had told him she had fainted, "Oh, yes," he said, "and have you seen her since?"

Olivia hesitated, "I have talked with Blanche," she answered. "The doctor has put her to bed. She needs a protracted rest."

Taken aback, he had asked, "A rest, a rest from what?" He had thought with Blanche at hand, she took life very easily.

Olivia said, nonetheless, she had gone to bed, and that moreover there was a trained nurse taking care of her.

"A trained nurse?" he inquired.

"Yes," she had said. "It was very mysterious, very mysterious indeed."

THE NEXT morning before going to the office, he visited his mother.

She had had a bad night, and the nurse was bringing her her breakfast before she had a chance to erase as much as possible the devastating marks of pain and fatigue that lined her face. Her hair had been hastily arranged, and the appearance she presented could scarcely persuade anyone that she was not seriously ill.

He had entered her room just as the light breakfast table was laid across her knees, and the nurse was assisting her to sit erect against her pillows.

Startled by his intrusion, she had looked up. "Why David," she cried, "I didn't know that you were back."

It was apparent that she was unprepared to meet the situation that confronted her.

"And I didn't know that you were ill," he had said, stooping to kiss her forehead.

"But I am not ill. Olivia must have told you. The doctor has insisted on my taking a little rest. There's no more to it than that, my darling." She took his hand and smiled up into his face.

The nurse told her she must eat her breakfast, with a look that completely disavowed the statement her patient had just made.

Suddenly, love for his mother and the fear of losing her enveloped him in an ancient memory—the sound of crashing breakers, the awful accumulation of his fears convulsed him. Throwing himself into his mother's arms and aware of the dreaded presence at her side, he heard the compelling voice of passion and persuasion gradually, and at her command, dissolving into the pure element of her love and sacrifice. And looking into her altered face, it seemed to him that the only thing that mattered was that his mother could be restored to him in full possession of her health and the great bounty of her unfailing love.

Seeing then that Blanche had entered and was managing the situation with her usual efficiency, he turned to her for the reassurance that he craved.

"Why, David," she said, dismissing the nurse, "we didn't know that you were back." And doing her best to disguise the lies that she was telling him, said he musn't be alarmed. They were merely giving his mother a rest the doctor had recommended.

And if he had asked about her nurse, his mother added, it had been only on Blanche's willingness to procure one that she had obeyed the arbitrary orders. She had not wished to put over on her and on old Norah the burden of carrying up and down the stairs so many trays and other necessities.

Happy to have his apprehensions considerably relieved, he sat down while his mother ate her breakfast, and presently the conversation turned on his trip to Boston and the work he had accomplished, and he found himself caught again in the lies and subterfuges in which his pursuit of Helen had entangled him. Little David had departed for New Hampshire. He would join Olivia there as soon as possible.

His mother's face had meanwhile become so animated by her interest and affection that he was willing to accept Blanche's version of her condition. He remained till she had finished her breakfast and the nurse had reappeared to take the tray downstairs. And after further conversation, he departed for his office.

On his way downtown he resolved not to telephone the Plaza or attempt the slightest interference with Helen's plans, but to let the days go by until some event that he had not himself provoked would make another meeting necessary.

A week elapsed without his hearing from her or even knowing whether or not she had returned to town, and he was beginning to feel that sanity had gained a victory over the madness that had so long obsessed him, when one evening after dinner, Olivia told him that she had sent a letter of condolence and some flowers to his friend at the Plaza and had had a very nice note from her in response.

Surprised and taken off his guard, he had said appreciatively that it was very nice of her to have sent the flowers, and hesitating a moment, added that he did not know that she was back.

Olivia, though she looked surprised, appeared to act as though he had told the truth. After a moment's silence, and looking at him with her earnest, humorless eyes, added, with great solemnity, that she was aware of his infatuation for Miss Brooks but that it had not too much disturbed her because she was sure that this was an illness from which he would presently recover. The silence still unbroken, she continued with increasing earnestness—she would, if she could, assist him to recover, but she must wait, and while she was waiting, she wanted him to know that she had perfect trust in him and in his love and loyalty to little David and to herself.

He had listened with growing irritation. The faith she assured him that she placed upon his loyalty, without, he knew, the slightest knowledge of the anguish he was undergoing in his attempts to subdue his passion for Helen Brooks, angered him. An illness from which she knew he would recover! The words revolted him. She might have said his illness was, and had been for many years, an attempt to adjust to a virtuous, entirely humorless, complacent woman and that his need for Helen Brooks had been the natural cry of his essential being, demanding love and the fulfillment of his desires.

Unable to answer her, he allowed her to enjoy her own words in protracted silence, presently excused himself, and going upstairs to his library, telephoned the Plaza. Had Miss Brooks returned, he inquired, and in an instant heard the beloved voice.

"David!" she had cried with warmth and real affection, "I had been expecting you to call."

He answered, and his voice was trembling with emotion, that he had waited to give her time to grow more accustomed to her sorrow before intruding on it.

But, she protested, she had wanted to see him and to thank him again for all he had done for them in Boston.

"When will you see me?" he had asked her humbly.

"Whenever you can come, my dear," she answered back.

Forgetting all other obligations, he asked if tomorrow at eleven would be convenient.

"Yes," she had said, "tomorrow at eleven, then."

On the following morning, he left the house before Olivia had come down for breakfast, and how he had spent the next three hours, the old gentleman was quite unable to remember. But with what emotion he remembered that meeting in the little parlor overlooking Central Park.

She had never seemed to him more beautiful or more remote. Her mourning and the sorrow in her face seemed, at the same time that it removed her from him, to have made him feel the necessity of reaching her, of coming to her aid. She had greeted him with warmth and gratitude, and after they had shaken hands and were seated opposite each other she had begun immediately, with that frankness that he had always loved in her, to take him into her confidence and had discussed with him the plans and problems that confronted her.

She was trying, she said, to forget her own bereavement in being of some comfort to poor old Bobby, who had been, she told him, completely shattered by his loss. He had decided to join her father and herself in Europe as soon as he could wind up his business connections in America. He and her father had always been more at home in Europe than in this country.

As he listened, fear, horror was at his heart. To think of her, the only one of the beautiful trio, left to trail about Europe with the two somewhat dubious gentlemen in whose society he had first beheld her.

And suddenly he was protesting eagerly, impetuously. She must not think of her father and of Mr. Gunn but of herself. There was one thing he knew would give her comfort and that was to go to China to see her other sister. This, and he took her hand in his, was what she should decide to do.

But, she had given a rueful laugh, how could that be possible? She was dependent on her father. She had no jewels she could sell, no money in the bank. Her father would not hear of such a plan.

He could control his passion no longer. He told her that he loved her, that she must not, he would not allow her to go to Europe. He could make arrangements for her; he would see to it that she got to China, she must put her trust in him, she must let him take care of all her plans.

She snatched her hand from his and put her face between her hands. "Oh, David, don't," she said. "Please," she cried, "I cannot bear it," and he saw a bright tear fall between her fingers.

He heard a key in the lock, and then he saw that her father and Mr. Gunn were entering the room. They were dressed in conspicuous mourning and their greeting was very friendly. They thanked him profusely for all that he had done for them in Boston. How could they have got on without him?

Hardly knowing how to acknowledge their thanks or how to make an exit, he said that he was on the point of leaving and that he must depart, and bidding them all good morning, left the room.

What had he said to Helen? How had she responded to him?

To FORGET ALL fidelities, save to the woman he adored, had now become his pattern of behavior. Not knowing just what he had told Helen when he had been interrupted by the entrance of her father and Mr. Gunn, he was not deterred from trying to carry out his reckless, well-nigh impossible schemes. Her sorrow and the distress he knew she was experiencing in planning to depart for Europe gave him a desperate sense that he must play for time, that he must intervene. He prepared himself to be ready for any emergency, acquainting himself with the dates of every ocean liner sailing for China from either San Francisco or Seattle. He engaged passage on each steamer scheduled to depart from either port, for the next two months.

Awaiting eventualities, he found it difficult to carry on his day-to-day existence. He regulated all the decision that had to be made by the urgent intentions that occupied his mind. He disregarded all Olivia's demands upon him, and he allowed Blanche's reassurances about his mother to persuade him he had no further reason to worry about her health. Days passed without his visiting her again. He forgot all obligations to little David and every weekend retracted his promise to go with Olivia to New Hampshire.

Meanwhile he found his visits to the Plaza more and more frustrating and yielding him greater cause for anxiety.

Although Helen seemed to have chosen him among her other admirers as the only one she cared to see, she was scarcely ever alone with him, for she was usually accompanied by either her father or Robert Gunn. And on the rare occasions he was alone with her, she showed a firm determination to keep him at a distance. If he could only know just what he had said to her that morning when his passionate outburst had been so suddenly interrupted! Did she know that he was ready to assist her in visiting her sister, or could it have been possible he had never spoken the words that his mind had framed for him? Sometimes he felt she recognized in him the only person who could save her from her intolerable decision, and that this coolness toward him was merely a sign of desires she was struggling to subdue.

Time was running short. Her father's plans had not been divulged, but he was afraid that their passage had been engaged for Europe, and though he did not know the date on which they planned to sail, he knew that it was imminent and that he had but little time to carry out his plans. It was late in June, the season was advanced and the warm days—the breath of summer in the city streets—increased the urgency of his desires.

Then came the morning, sitting in his office overlooking the blue waters of the bay, when he resolved at any cost to divulge his plans to Helen and discover just how matters stood with her. Every moment that he waited, he was in danger of losing her forever.

Gazing at the busy traffic in the harbor, he answered absentmindedly a knock on his door. And when his secretary entered to tell him a young lady was outside and waiting to see him, a rush of absurd and sudden joy invaded him. Could it be possible that this was Helen? Had she come to tell him of her plight, to ask his advice? But when the door opened he looked up to see that Blanche was coming toward him.

"Oh, Blanche," he had said, trying to disguise his disappointment but nonetheless looking with obvious disapproval at her. "What brings you all the way down here?"

She had looked at him with grave, reproachful eyes.

He hadn't too much time, he'd said, looking at his watch and waving her to a seat. He had been so caught up in the details of this case that he was on that he hardly had a moment he could call his own.

She had seated herself, without removing her clear and penetrating gaze, and he saw in her truthful eyes all the candor and confidence of their childhood and knew that what she expected of him at this moment was fidelity to their old, implicit honesties. He knew she knew that he was lying. When she went on to say, quite disregardful of his explanation and making it perfectly clear to him that she was well acquainted with the truth, that she had come to break a solemn secret she had made to his mother, he denied the right she had to tell him and said he would wait until he heard the secret from her himself. Fighting his desire to tell her to go away, he added that he knew he had been neglectful and would do his best to call upon her as soon as he could find the time. And then yielding to his unfriendly impulse, he rose as though to say their interview was over.

But Blanche had had no intention of being thus rudely dismissed. "David," she had cried, and in her face he saw such condemnation and rebuke, he had quailed before her gaze. With no attempt to spare him she had told him fiercely that his mother was fatally ill, and the fact that he had not had sufficient insight to see that she was dying had been the reason she had come. Moreover, she had continued, his mother's heart was breaking because of her concern for him and his heartless neglect of her. Then, while he waited, she had changed her tone, and pleading with him, had said, "Come with me now to see her, David. It would mean so much, for in the morning she has greater strength than later on."

"Quite impossible," he had answered firmly, adding that he would come the first moment he could find the time to do so. Without another word she left him, and stricken by his own behavior, he sat down and placed his hands before his face.

Why in God's name had she so angered him! Struggling against his fear that what she had said was true, he tried to put his faith in his mother's assurances and to forget how long it was since he had seen her. He did his best to make out that Blanche had tried deliberately to alarm him. And deeply resentful of being forced at this crucial moment to face two impending crises—his mother's imminent death and Helen's imminent departure—he made up his mind to go without delay to the Plaza.

Out on the street he looked about him, undetermined still, plagued by the thought of his brusque behavior to Blanche and by self-reproach at his neglect of his mother and by his increasing fear that Blanche's news was true; he hailed a cab.

Looking at the crowds, the familiar streets and passing the landmarks that he knew so well, memories intruded, a gentleman with a dark beard, his mother underneath a street lamp, a kiss exchanged, and then the haunting syllables "Louise Denis, Louise Denis" taken up and repeated by the revolution of the wheels.

Arrived at the hotel, he dismissed the cab and doing his best to master his emotions, inquired at the desk if Miss Brooks would be able to see him and after waiting several moments for a reply, learned that she was in and wished him to come up.

Ascending in the elevator, he prayed desperately that he

would find her alone, and arriving at her door, waited for a response.

At last his knock was answered by an unfamiliar voice and on entering, he found a young Irish woman, who told him that the lady would be in directly.

Looking about for a place to sit, he saw that everything was in complete disarray. An open steamer trunk was partially packed. Bulging bags already strapped and tagged were in a corner. Dresses were thrown across the backs of chairs. In the midst of all this confusion the Irish girl stood regarding him, and as she repeated her assurance that the lady would be in, he heard Helen calling to him from her bedroom that she was coming in an instant.

So much evidence of an immediate departure alarmed him and rendered him incapable of knowing what to do from one moment to the next. And as he was all but telling the servant to get out, Helen appeared in the doorway. Telling the maid, before addressing him, to lift the tray from the trunk and place it on the floor, she came forward, greeting him and bidding him to forgive the mess in which he found himself. Then, apparently determined not to dismiss her, she ordered the maid to go into the bedroom and find her steamer rug and heavy coat, and if they had been brushed, to bring them back and she would tell her what to do with them.

The maid departed, leaving the door between the rooms ajar. Doing his utmost to control his impulse to rush to Helen and take her in his arms, he restrained himself and went instead to close the door.

They faced each other then. "Were you intending to depart," he asked her coldly, "without so much as telling me when you were sailing?"

"I'm afraid I was," she said, in a voice so low that he could hardly catch what she had said.

"By God," he answered, snatching her, taking her roughly in his arms, "I will not let you go. You cannot play this trick on me." Then suddenly he felt her lips against his own and the gradual relaxing of her resistance to him.

"David," she cried. "David, don't."

He felt, he knew that every nerve and fiber in her body was responding to his passion. "My love, my darling, my beloved," he cried, and suddenly aware that she was struggling against him, he made a desperate effort to keep her in his arms.

"Let me go, for God's sake, let me go, David," she ordered, pushing him away, and managing finally to release herself, backed away from him and stood against the wall, crying out in a great rage, "It was my fault," she sobbed, "I should never have let you come."

"So," he retorted fiercely, "it was your intention to escape without so much as telling me that you were going?"

"Yes," she said, "but when they told me at the desk that you were here, I don't know, I can't tell you just what happened to me from that moment to this, I thought that I could see it through."

"You can't," he cried. "By God, you can't." And at that moment there was a knock at the door, and the maid, carrying the coat and the steamer rug, returned, saying they were well brushed and asking what Miss Brooks wished her to do with them now. With a great effort at self-control, she took the coat from her, packed it in the trunk amid the books and shoes and assisting her in lifting the tray from the floor, closed the trunk and taking the steamer rug, went with it to the corner and threw it down amid the pile of bulging luggage.

Incapable of rendering assistance but seeing an opportunity to intervene, he told the maid, with quite unauthorized authority, that Miss Brooks would have no further need of her just now. She went out at once, and he closed the door behind her.

But Helen rushed from the corner and opening it called, "Come back, Hannah, come back."

Apparently she had not heard. Closing the door again, he stood confronting her. They were both agitated. She implored him to leave her. She could not bear, she said, the anguish of bidding him good-bye. She crossed the room.

He followed her and told her passionately that there would be no good-byes. Ordering her to listen to him, he repeated that there would be no good-byes.

She closed her eyes. "Please, David, please," she pleaded. "I cannot stand it."

"Oh, yes you can, my dear," he answered fiercely, bidding her listen to him and do exactly what he told her. They had little time to lose.

What did he mean, she demanded, opening her eyes.

"I mean that you are not sailing off to Europe tomorrow or the next day. You are going on a voyage with me, across another ocean. I am taking you to China. That is where you said you wanted most to go."

She told him he was mad and asked if he had gone quite off his head.

"I am in complete possession of my faculties. Listen to me," he commanded roughly. "Do exactly what I tell you. Finish your packing, stick the labels on your trunks and boxes, have your suitcase locked and labeled, keep your head and manage to disguise your perturbation. Then when you see that nothing is suspected, get out of here. Leave this place forever. You needn't change your clothes, and you mustn't take a coat or bag or parcel with you. Come to me as soon as you can contrive it. Remember this: I should be at the Murray Hill Hotel by five o'clock. If I am not there, wait for me. But if I am, ask for the number of Mr. Henry Harvey's room and come up to me directly."

She said she would not, she could not possibly agree to such a scheme.

"Why on God's earth can't you?" he demanded.

She would not ruin his career. She would not deprive him of his child. He could not ignore his future or forget his obligations.

She could give him sons and daughters, he declared with vehemence.

Perhaps, she said, that might be so. But wherever they might be together, he would be known as the Mr. Hare who had once eloped with a young woman by the name of Helen Brooks. How long would he continue to adore her?

He asked her if she did not think he had dwelt on these questions. Either she came with him, or if she did not . . .

Such a suggestion was not worthy of him, she scornfully declared.

There was the sound of a latch key in the door and the voices of Mr. Gunn and Helen's father. "Where are you, Helen?" they cried as they entered, both of them demanding her attention. And then aware of his presence, stopped abruptl .

"Our good friend David!" Robert Gunn exclaimed, slapping him warmly on the shoulder.

They both said they were glad that he had come, and turning to Helen, asked if she had broken the news of their departure.

"The evidence is all about me," she had answered, gallantly attempting to laugh.

Robert suggested a drink, a toast to their successful voyage.

"No,' he answered, looking not at them but straight

at Helen. He had not the time, but he would be at the steamer to see them off.

"And we'll drink to our reunion, when you come to Paris," added Helen, and the steady glance she gave him intimated—what, he wondered. She was certainly obeying his commands to keep her head and show no sign of perturbation.

Mr. Brooks escorted him to the door. "Good-bye," they all called back, "until tomorrow at the steamer."

Walking to the elevator down the wide corridor of the hotel, he recaptured her steady gaze. Good God, he muttered, so little time, so much to do. First to the bank to procure sufficient funds to finance this stupendous business. Then to his office, where he would write Olivia. He would not go home. He could travel with clothes he wore upon his back. He would buy a razor and shaving brush. That would be sufficient. If he remembered rightly, there was a train leaving the Grand Central for Chicago at 8:00 P.M. Would she come or would she not? Was he filled with fear or exultation?

The night was changing to the gray of dawn, and old Miss Willoughby had awakened and was thinking of David and of that visit she had made him at the office. "Yes, yes," she whispered, "I have forgiven you. Ten thousand times, was what I told you, David." And she remembered then the afternoon he had eloped with Helen.

Laura had just had an injection of morphia and of greater strength than usually allowed. The merciful narcotic had taken a strong hold. And hardly able to believe in her release from pain and fearing lest this ineffable bliss might at any moment escape, she lay back against her pillows, relaxed and sighing gratefully. Smiling, she'd said how glad she was that she was with her now. And presently asked if she had seen David since that day he had come to see them after his return from Boston.

Hoping to be forgiven, she told her that she had not. And she added that she was afraid she'd spoken to him far too casually about her illness. But then, she must remember she had done her best to keep her promise. She felt herself that he had been too long without another visit. He would have come more often had he the slightest idea of how ill she was.

He had not, she understood, gone to New Hampshire to see little David.

She believed he had not.

Poor David, she had always known that if he ever fell in love something violent and destructive was likely to occur. But then there was little David, and she counted on his affection for the boy.

At this point they were interrupted by the entrance of the nurse, and Laura had told her that the morphia had worked beautifully. She was grateful for the relief—she felt no pain at all.

"Thank God for that!" The nurse took Laura's pulse, and nodding, said that everything was satisfactory. She must try to get a little sleep. A nice long nap would do her worlds of good.

Laura had protested and said that she felt no desire to sleep. She wished to stay awake that she might enjoy the perfect bliss of her relief from pain.

And so the nurse went out, and she had suggested that she need not return until she rang for her.

Laura smiled her approval and said again that she was so glad to have her beside her.

She had asked if Laura wished to continue their conversation, or should they speak of something else?

She had smiled and said they would speak of happier things. They shared so many memories from which to choose a few that would delight them both.

Then she had said that cousin Laura had hit on a delightful thought. She knew just where to start.

Old Miss Willoughby closed her eyes. Voices, voices, laughter of children, shadows of the young leaves on the paths and on the grass, a spring day—twittering of sparrows near the tulip tree; boys on roller skates and little Olivia Wildering with two long pigtails down her back; Lily in a dress just like her own, and David's mother on her usual bench.

Laura, pale and smiling against her pillows urged her to go on.

She had told her then of the first day she had ever noticed her. She was sitting on her bench reading a book and didn't even know that she was there. She had climbed onto the bench beside her. She could not possibly describe her agitation and excitement when finally she had turned to her and said, "Who are you?" Her heart was beating so fast that she never knew how she had had the courage to say that she was Blanche Willoughby. And when she'd said, "Willoughby, Willoughby, why, you must be David's cousin," her surprise and happiness were not to be described.

How gently her dear Laura had placed her thin hand in her own. "And from that moment," she had said, "my little Blanche and I began to share our memories of that lovely vanished park."

The spring, they both agreed, had been the happiest season there, when the marbles and tops appeared, the skipping ropes and hoops, the new straw hats and the light coats; there was the day the fountain was turned on and the day that Mr. Pierson's bull arrived. What a wonderful, happy place it had been, the games, the fights and friendships, the secret conversations of the little girls, the boys dashing madly about on roller skates. Everything so vivid and full of life, even the calamities exciting. The day Louisa Ware fell into the fountain, and the day Emmet Harris broke his collar bone, and the bloodcurdling moment when Mr. Pierson's bull charged the nurses and the baby carriages and Olivia stood her ground and challenged him to come on.

Here Laura interrupted and said she had never been able to congratulate Olivia for that courageous deed. There had been something so self-satisfied about her as though to say, well why not, what else could she have done?

And then they both remembered her behavior at the birthday party, standing there in her simple white dress amid all that magnificence, greeting her little friends with the politeness and good manners of a perfect hostess. There they all were in that great marble hall with the fountain and the flowers and the flunkies and that magician flinging about his rabbits and canary birds. With what awe and admiration they had been filled; silent, unnaturally subdued until that unique opportunity to chase the birds and rabbits had released them to free expression of their joy in all that magic.

The enchanting scene came back. They saw, they felt it all—the children flying off in every direction, screaming with joy, laughing, calling to each other. David dancing off with Olivia, bemused but proud to be her chosen partner.

And old Blanche knew, as they rehearsed it, that Laura was thinking of that moment on Park Avenue when a gentleman with a pointed beard had approached the little flock she shepherded and greeting her, had kissed her hand, and she had answered as he left them, "Until Thursday at the Warings', then."

But what she loved the most, she had continued, had been the family dinners. And presently they both were launched upon the memories of those festival occasions, the gala table decorations, Christmases and Easters, the familiar characters—Cousin Lucy, little Mr. Friedermann, Agatha, Great-aunt Adelaide, and outrageous Uncle Alex. While she, no, she must not deny it, had pulled the strings and set the scenes and conversations going, just, it had always seemed to her, for David's special benefit.

And later in the drawing room—how vividly it all came back—sitting on the sofa next to David, while they listened to the "Little Night Piece." "Eine Kleine Nachtmusik," yes, they both agreed, it had been the theme song of David's childhood. With its loveliness and grace and gaiety; how he had delighted in it!

And there was, she had asked her if she remembered, one dinner that stood out among the others—an Easter Sunday, the daffodils, the freesia on the table filling the heart with spring, the conversation fascinating, Uncle Alex at his outrageous best. And did she recollect the remark he'd made about the Wilderings and Jesus Christ and how he talked with Great-aunt Adelaide about the Paris nephews and had asked David what could be done about the Hares and David's quick suggestion that they'd better set the hounds on them?

Watching Laura, she had asked her if she could tell her why it was that Uncle Alex had always so heartily disliked the Wilderings. But still regarding her, she had seen she was not listening. "Are you asleep?" she had whispered, in a voice that indicated she did not expect an answer.

"No, dear," she had answered. She was wide awake. She had been lying here quite happy. She had been thinking of David, wondering where he was and what he was doing and wishing he would drop in to make a little call.

"He might just do that," she had answered.

It would be the perfect moment, she had said, while she was so comfortable and unaware of pain. "What time is it?" she had asked abruptly.

Looking at her watch, she'd answered, "It's just on five, my dearest."

As THE OLD gentleman got into the taxi and gave the address to the driver, he was thinking of Blanche.

Dear girl, he thought, how she had loved his mother, how loyal she had always been! And he pictured her as he had known her long ago. Beautiful? he queried. Yes, with her finely chiseled features and her large dark eyes so full of eloquence, of speech, he corrected himself, for he had always felt he knew of what she thought when she was speaking. And remembering the last time he had seen her, he wondered now at her forgiveness given so readily and with such apparent joy.

How much, he wondered, had she known about his life with Helen? Certainly she knew that she was dead. Possibly she had guessed something of the anguish she had caused him, chasing about with her from one place to another, exhibiting her charms, applauding her wit—the most delighted, it would appear, of her admirers—jealous, cursing himself out for the humiliations that she imposed upon him, longing to be free of her and of her infidelities. But after she was gone, and he was free—how gladly he would have endured the habitual torments for the enchantment of her presence, the sound of her lovely laughter.

Approaching his destination, he wondered why, since the world had undergone such changes—initiations—wholesale tragedies, he should be entitled to fix his thoughts for the past two days and nights exclusively upon his life, his passions, his loyalties, and his betrayals.

But here he was on Blanche's doorstep. He opened the door and found himself in the hallway of an old-fashioned house. Looking up the three flights of stairs and taking a long breath, he began laboriously to climb them. Arriving at the third floor, he found the door wide open and Mrs. Drew waiting to let him in.

"Miss Willoughby is in the living room," she said, "waiting your arrival with impatience."

Giving her his hat and overcoat, he walked into the large bright room, and there rising to meet him with both hands extended was Blanche. It did not seem to him that she had changed, in spite of the fact that her hair was white as snow and that the expression of her face revealed the experience and the discipline of over fifty years. He read in her expression all that old and beautiful fidelity to Laura and the love for him on which that greater love was nourished. The blame and the bitterness she had felt for him for many years had been erased.

They did not speak but stood for some time clasping each other's hands and looking deep into each other's eyes.

The past engulfed them—vibrations of the nerves connecting memory with memory, instantaneous transport from childhood to youth to maturity; they seemed to be moving together from place to place, from scene to scene, from year to year. Places, rooms wherein momentous conversations had been exchanged, faces of the dead reanimated by thoughts of them, moments, moments, the appearance and disappearance of familiar presences, sounds, fragrances.

To Mrs. Drew, who stood regarding them, their silence became intolerable. Miss Willoughby had neither kissed nor spoken to the boyfriend. What was the meaning of such curious behavior? Finally she said, forgetful of Blanche's previous injunctions, "I expect you'd like to give the gentleman a cup of tea."

"No," Blanche said, dropping David's hands and looking at her with great severity, "I think I told you, we will have no tea," adding that she would have no further need of her.

Meanwhile, David, too much moved for conversation, went to the window and looked out, while Blanche reseated herself and allowed the silence to continue.

A boy on the rooftops was flying pigeons, and the belfry of Our Lady of Pompeii lifted its cross against the western sky. As he looked at the humble church in its Italian neighborhood, at the low roofs and the wide skyscape, the long years of his exile rushed upon him—his love for Helen, his anguish at her infidelities, her grave at Davos, where she had lain beside her mother for thirty years, his sorrow at her loss. How much, he wondered again, had Blanche known about his life with Helen. She seemed in some extraordinary way to have become his mother, as though she were waiting just as Laura used to wait on her bench in their old playground for him to come to her to weep his heart out after injuries he had sustained.

He felt sure that she would not be the first one to break the long-protracted silence. And not quite ready to go directly to her, he left the window, and going to the low bookcases lined up against her wall, began to examine her books. Suddenly he stopped, and inspecting the titles of three uniformly bound volumes (*The Influence of the Italian Masters on the Paintings of the Dutch, A Study of Memling, An Approach to the Italian Renaissance*), broke the silence by asking her if she had read them all.

She responded immediately, beckoning him to come and sit beside her on the sofa.

He went to her at once, and for some time they talked

quite impersonally of art and of his books and the pleasure she had had in reading them.

But then overwhelmed by the memories to which his heart was open, he fell to his knees and laid his head in Blanche's lap.

As she waited for him to speak, it seemed to her that she was Laura, that she was his mother into whose arms she had often seen him run, emptying his heart of tears and all his childish woes; but realizing that his silence was his only means of expressing all that he craved to say, she answered him with silence, she knew that each could hear the other speak.

No need to tell his story—his regrets, his accumulating griefs, the long years of readjustment, moving aimlessly about from place to place, the intolerable memories, all this came to her direct from him.

The silence became too loud. There was in this communion too much, too many echoes from the past. Louise Denis (was it Louis, was it Louise?)—the name moved like the dominant motif of his appeal for her forgiveness, recalling to her the morning she had come to implore him to visit Laura, and his abandonment that very evening of her and of his little son, whom he had never seen again.

The silence that had protected them from the violation of the spoken word, she at last deliberately broke, speaking to him with gentleness of little David, whom she had known and loved. He had been, she said, an exceptional young man and had come to see her often for the sole purpose of learning all she could tell him about his father. Aware of the attention with which he listened to her, she knew at once how comforting her words had been. She watched him lift his head and then she waited.

He asked her abruptly if it was possible the boy had

borne him no ill will for the abominable manner in which he had deserted him and his poor mother.

"No, no, David," she answered gently, as, with great difficulty, for he was old and stiff and found it extremely painful to get up from his knees, he rose and taking her hand, pressed it to his lips and seated himself beside her on the sofa. "Quite the contrary," she assured him. He had always been eager to hear everything about the mysterious parent who had vanished so unaccountably from his life. His memories of him, she explained, had been more like an atmosphere of joy and gaiety than of a human presence who had contributed these pleasures. But as he grew older, throughout his youth and early manhood, he had wished to discover for himself the actual father the mention of whose existence had been so scrupulously avoided all his life and about whom he had only been able to conjecture. He had conceived the idea of going to Paris to discover him.

What, he asked her, had prevented the boy from coming? God knows, he would have welcomed him with joy.

It had taken but four words after his announcement of his plan to Olivia for him to relinquish his long-cherished hope.

What had she said to him?

"Let bygones be bygones."

"Poor Olivia!"

Blanche laid her hand on David's. "Poor Olivia," she repeated.

Had the boy loved his mother? David finally questioned her.

Yes, she said, after a moment's hesitation, she thought so. He admired the way she never asked for sympathy or listened to either gossip or criticism. He had been willing to give up his passionate desire to go in search of him rather than do anything to disturb the courage and complacency with which she consistently endeavored to conceal her broken heart.

And now again the rush of memories—the need for silence. But when they felt that they had plumbed the wells of these old tragedies, David, changing the climate of their communion, in a voice that seemed to plead for happier moods and recollections, asked rather wryly what she had told the boy about him.

"Oh, many things," she answered, laughing. How charming he had been and witty.

And finally they were in the midst of recalling their most cherished memories—the outrageous Uncle Alex and his derision of Laura for insisting he was born to be a poet, the chatter and chaff around the festive table, and Laura, who used to pull the strings of conversation for his special delectation, making the relatives display their most beguiling foibles and eccentricities.

And all at once old Miss Willoughby and old David Hare entered the vanished playground of their childhood— there was Laura's special bench beneath the tulip tree, the place under the willows where the little girls told secrets, and the section of the walk which the little boys had made their private property, the games and the fights and the constant sense that something dramatic and exciting was about to happen. Was it a day in October, when the air smelled of the cold weather and the fallen leaves, or was it winter, when the little boys wore heavy reefers and the little girls were dressed in woolen coats and mittens, or was it a spring afternoon when the trees were full of bursting buds and opening leaves and feathery blossoms and the sparrows were exceptionally noisy in the air and in the boughs of the trees, when the voices of the children were tuned to all the various enterprises that the season had set afoot, when the fountain that had just been turned on was plashing and plunging, and the bull was back in his usual quarters, and Laura sat upon her accustomed bench, and Olivia had just been deposited by her grandfather and was entering the park by the northeast gate, and the all but forgotten sound of rumbling carriage wheels and horses hitting the pavements with their hoofs continued without interruption?

Laura closed her book. Olivia drove off with Mr. Wildering. David and Blanche prepared to go home. And while Mrs. Drew watched the two old people through an opening of the kitchen door, their memories still invading them, the rumbling of the ancient vehicles continuing—the immense panorama of the years behind them with its miraculous inventions and achievements, its terrible wars with their incredible paraphernalia, their vast terrestrial, oceanic, and aerial arenas passed rapidly before them, moving it would seem (and oh! they prayed together, might love and reverence for life prevail) toward some immense, annihilating, and unimaginable catastrophe.